A FORMER CHURCH OF SCOTLAND PARISH MINISTER, Ron Ferguson is now a full-time writer. From 1990 to 2001 he was minister of St Magnus Cathedral in Kirkwall. Living in Orkney, he is a regular columnist and book reviewer with both *The Herald* and the *Press and Journal*, and has twice been a runner up for Columnist of the Year in the Bank of Scotland Press Awards. He was shortlisted for the McVities Scottish Writer of the Year Award for his biography of George MacLeod.

RON FERGUSON

The Reluctant Reformation of Clarence McGonigall

Steve Savage
LONDON AND EDINBURGH

Steve Savage Publishers Ltd
The Old Truman Brewery
91 Brick Lane
LONDON
E1 6QL

www.savagepublishers.com

Published in Great Britain by Steve Savage Publishers Ltd 2003

ISBN 1-904246-09-5

British Library Cataloguing in Publication Data
A catalogue entry for this book is available from the British Library

Earlier versions of most of these stories were published in *Life & Work*
in 2002 and 2003, and publishers wish to express their gratitude to
Life & Work for permission to use the stories in this volume.

Typeset by Steve Savage Publishers Ltd
Printed and bound by The Cromwell Press Ltd

Contents

Foreword

The Reverend J. Clarence McGonigall has acquired a special place in the hearts of *Life & Work* readers. Initially commissioned as a single story in a brilliant flash of inspiration by the magazine's Interim Editor, Dr Harry Reid, it was quickly apparent the rebel curmudgeon had struck a chord with the people in the pews.

The Clarence chronicles were extended to three, then six and then finally twelve, covering the final year in the ministry of the cantankerous churchman whose struggles with the demands of modern ministry and whose refusal to 'toe the line' in the fictitious Presbyterian Church (Scotland) caused uproarious laughter in homes across the nation every month.

But it is not just Church of Scotland members who have been entertained by Clarence's adventures and mishaps in the imaginary Presbyterian church of the future. *Life & Work* readers have reported outbreaks of hilarity among friends and family of all ages following the latest instalment of the Reverend McGonigall's.

So what is his appeal? Perhaps he represents the sense of longing that is inside all of us not to conform with authority. Sometimes also less than perfect, he is human in his failings, but equally endearing in his goodness and frequently frustrated search for his ideal church.

It is a tribute to the talent and skill of Ron Ferguson, a fellow Fifer, that readers have come to believe Clarence must be based on a real person, possibly even Ron himself. While there are one or two similarities, e.g. both ministers have owned dogs named Squeegee, I can assure followers the resemblance ends there and Clarence is indeed the work of a vividly fertile imagination.

Life & Work is delighted to have spawned such a runaway success and I hope readers enjoy this collection as much as I have enjoyed commissioning them.

Lynne Robertson
Editor, *Life & Work*
Spring 2003

Introduction

I must admit that the success of the Reverend J. Clarence McGonigall surprised me. What was supposed to be a one-off story took on a life of its own, and evolved into a year-long ecclesiastical soap opera.

It quickly became clear that the rebellious, cantankerous old minister was tapping into an unease in the manses and pews of the Kirk about the centralisation of power, and the attempts to fit ministry into a particular mould. So this batty, unmanageable cleric in the year 2009 began to haunt some contemporary feasts.

At dinner parties, people would ask me about Aggie and Squeegee. Readers, some of whom wrote fan mail to Clarence, and even wanted to run a campaign to make him Moderator, tried to identify real-life characters in the tales, and to suggest that the stories were 'really' about very contemporary issues. As the great philosopher-king Kenny Dalglish might have put it, 'Mibbes, aye, mibbes naw.'

The stories can be interpreted on a number of levels. (Well, let's not get carried away here. Maybe two levels. I'm not pretending to be the Chekhov of Cowdenbeath.) However, the tales are primarily ecclesiastical entertainments. If they amuse you, I will be pleased. If you find deeper meaning, then fine. Your deeper meaning may not be my deeper meaning, but, hey, we live in a post-modern age, so what's the problem?

I would like to thank Dr Harry Reid, former editor of the *Herald* and a journalistic mentor of mine, not only for writing the Afterword, but for commissioning the first stories; and Lynne Robertson, the editor of *Life & Work* not only for writing the Foreword, but for extending the Life of Clarence so supportively. Lynne was also very enthusiastic about this book, and readily granted permission to use the stories which had appeared in *Life & Work*. Other material has been written specially for this book.

Bill McArthur who, like me, lives in Orkney, is a superb illustrator. He deservedly received the accolade of 'Cartoonist of the Year' at the Scottish Press Awards last year.

Thanks also to my publisher, Steve Savage, for his support and commitment.

Ron Ferguson
Lent 2003

1. The Strange Promotion of Miss Araminta Pringle

He sat despondently in his study, surrounded by piles of paperwork. The stuff was on his desk, in piles on the floor, everywhere. Most of it had come from the Kirk's new custom-built headquarters in Livingston.

Things were so bad, he even yearned for the good old days of the former Church of Scotland's headquarters at 121 George Street, Edinburgh. He had never thought he would see that day.

For the Reverend J. Clarence McGonigall, minister of Inversnecky North, linked with Scunner South, linked with Trachle (Continuing), linked with Havers Memorial, the year of Our Lord 2009 brought no cheer. Two years after the privatisation of the Church of Scotland, things had simply got worse.

What bothered him most about the Kirk—or The Presbyterian Church (Scotland) as it was now known —was its relentless 'modernization' on marketing lines. The very thought of it made him weary. Next year he would retire, and it couldn't come soon enough.

The other thing Clarence couldn't abide was the pervasive church management-speak. Following a report by management consultants, the church had been broken up into three separate self-contained 'growth' divisions—baptisms, weddings and funerals —under the overall direction of a Chief Executive. The sale of 121 George Street and the Assembly Hall on the Mound had raised a substantial sum, which was used to fund the appointment of Regional Growth Directors.

Clarence had sighed when short-term contracts for ministers were introduced. His own ministries had each lasted for more than fifteen years, and he had felt he had only begun to get anywhere after the first seven years.

How he hated these endless retraining conferences addressed by enthusiastic young men who had themselves been trained in America! They spouted meaningless verbiage while endlessly grinning. It was all too much.

The avalanche of paper threatened to submerge him. Three-year reviews. Training manuals. Marketing tools. ('Clergypersons must identify their "product" and look at its selling points,' said one report.)

The final straw for Clarence had been the notion of payment by results. When he had first heard of the idea, he had been sure it was a spoof.

'Are we going to have targets for weddings and funerals?' he had joked to Aggie, his wife of forty years.

He joked too soon.

Clarence himself had been at the PC 'convention' in Livingston at which the matter was discussed. He felt completely out of his depth.

What used to be the Kirk's General Assembly had been turned into a bonding session for religious sales operatives. The metrical psalms, abandoned as 'yesterday's tunes', had been replaced by mind-numbing, sentimental, religious songs and choruses. The cringe-making words were displayed on large screens.

And the whole thing was so high-tech! Clarence felt like a dinosaur. Only once had he felt moved to speak— the very event rendered him speechless—and when he had stumbled to the microphone to make his protest against the new 'targets' system, he felt at a loss.

In order to activate the mike, he had to put a special electronic card in a slot. In his confusion, Clarence had put in his Visa card instead. The convention sniggered.

'These are the kind of people who are holding back progress in the church,' muttered one young teeshirt-wearing minister.

Payment by results was approved with acclaim.

'Not before time,' added the mutterer, looking towards Clarence.

A specially-bound PC report—recorded delivery— gave the instructions. 'Clergypersons' were given annual targets for baptisms, weddings and funerals. Ministers who met their targets by Easter would be rewarded by bonus payments of up to £1,000.

And that is when the trouble started.

'Clarence,' said Aggie plaintively, 'we need a new sofa. This one came out of the ark. It's falling to bits.'

Clarence hadn't noticed.

'We could pay it up,' added Aggie, knowing full well that her husband had never got into debt in his life. He would rather starve.

The minimum stipend had been reduced in recent years, to encourage ministers to work for the bonuses. Life was hard.

'Clarence,' went on Aggie plaintively, 'are you not due a bonus?'

Sitting helplessly in his study, Clarence reflected on how ministers had become functionaries. Bonuses! Still, he owed it to Aggie to check.

From the mound of papers from Livingston—all headed with The Presbyterian Church (Scotland)'s bright new yellow 'Mr Happy' logo—Clarence fished out a paper about bonuses. Eventually it dawned on him that he was only one short of his target for funerals.

Less than a week till Easter.

That very afternoon, he was due to visit Miss Pringle, a ninety-year-old parishioner who had been president of the Woman's Guild. She had also been the bane of the Reverend J. Clarence McGonigall's life. And she was poorly.

Clarence needed a drink. He poured himself a large dram, then put on his overcoat.

It was about half past four in the afternoon when the two policemen called at the manse. The younger one was embarrassed and apologetic. The older man, Sergeant Raymond Bunion, was a leading Baptist layman who had always regarded Presbyterians as soft on sin, and soft on the causes of sin.

'I'm sorry to trouble you, sir,' said the young policeman, 'but we need to ask you some questions about Miss Aramanta Pringle.'

'What about her?' asked the minister.

'I'm afraid, sir, that she's dead.'

'She can't be,' interjected Mr McGonigall, irrationally. 'I saw her only an hour or so ago, and she was alive.'

'You were the last one seen leaving the house,' said the older cop.

'You're not suggesting...' the minister's voice trailed away.

'I'm not suggesting anything, Mr McGonigall. But we have inquiries we must make.'

'Bloody officious Baptist,' muttered the minister, not quite under his breath.

'Sir, can I ask if you have been drinking?' asked the teetotal policeman.

'Only a dram. No, two drams. I had one when I came in. I always needed a dram after visiting that old battleaxe.'

'Oh,' said his interrogator, looking very grave, yet pleased with himself at the same time. 'Did you have reason to wish Miss Pringle dead?'

'Often,' replied the minister.

'Isn't it the case,' went on Bunion, 'that Presbyterian ministers have a bonus scheme? That if you reach your target, you'll be given more money?'

'Have you been reading seditious Presbyterian literature, Sergeant Bunion?' inquired the minister. 'Yes, I must admit, this lunacy has come from my church.'

'How many more funerals do you need in order to get your bonus?' inquired Clouseau McBunion, meaningfully.

'One.'

'I think, sir, you'd better come with us to the station.'

Aggie came in as they were leaving.

'What's going on?' she asked.

'The Baptist tendency wish to give me total immersion in the river. They have drugged me. Call the police. By the way, did you know that Miss Pringle is dead?'

'Does that mean we'll get our new sofa?' asked Aggie.

'Miss Pringle has been murdered, and I'm the chief suspect.'

'Oh, no,' said Aggie, a sob catching in her throat. 'I didn't want the sofa that badly.'

The two policemen looked at each other, then led the minister away.

The Reverend J. Clarence McGonigall was released the next day, without charge. DNA testing showed that blood spotted on the carpet belonged to Miss Pringle's nephew, who stood to inherit a lot of money.

Under pressure from his employers, the young man had got into deep financial trouble after being too ambitious with a couple of business deals. His aunt's money was coming to him anyway. She had always spoken longingly about heaven, so he decided to do her a favour by promoting her to glory more speedily than she had anticipated.

The funeral took place on a grey Good Friday. Clarence gave Miss Pringle a kindly and generous sendoff. Although she had given him a hard time, he knew that judgment belonged with God, not with him.

The following Monday evening, Clarence stood up decisively in the middle of the television news, and switched off the set.

With a determined look on his face, he marched purposefully through to the study, and gathered up all the papers on his desk and his study floor. He set down the papers in piles on the living room floor, and one by one put them on the fire, laughing manically.

Then he poured himself a dram, sat down, and put his arm around Aggie, on their lovely new sofa.

2. The Grave Sound of Nanny Kirk

It was half past eight in the morning when the telephone rang in Clarence McGonigall's study in Scunner manse.

'Not already!' he exclaimed to his dog, Squeegee, while putting his coffee cup back down on his desk.

'This is Nancy Kirk here, Mr McGonigall,' said the caller. 'I have something important to say to you.'

Clarence groaned under his breath. The Reverend Nancy Kirk was chief executive of the Presbyterian Church (Scotland), and a right busybody she was, earning herself the whispered soubriquet 'Nanny' Kirk. Her deputy, the Reverend Tanya Hyde—called 'Nanny Second' because of her tendency to echo her boss at the speed of sound—was in charge of whipping ministers into line, and keeping them 'on message'.

'All our ministers except you, Mr McGonigall, have a mobile phone. You have resisted our suggestions that you should have one. At headquarters, we need to be able to be in touch quickly with all our staff. Can you give me a good reason why you should not have a mobile?'

'Precisely because you want to get in touch with me quickly,' replied Clarence. 'That's as good a reason as any for not having one of these wretched things. Not only that, mobile phones are a pestilential nuisance.'

'I can see that you have not made any new year resolutions, Mr McGonigall. You are determined to remain your old intransigent self. Well, I have news for you. We have decided that you will have a mobile phone.'

'Who is "we", may I ask?'

'The Council,' replied Nancy Kirk.

'Oh, the Star Chamber,' said Clarence. 'You know, I can still remember the days when our Kirk was Presbyterian. I can even remember the days when dissent wasn't necessarily dismissed as disloyalty. John Knox would have been out on his lug in today's Presbyterian Church.'

Clarence had publicly opposed the establishment of the powerful 'Council of Seven' which had been set up following yet another review by management consultants. He had cited the almost-forgotten 'Church Without Walls' report of 2001 which had argued for less centralised control of the church. He had been told he was resisting the Holy Spirit.

The chairman of the Council was 32-year-old Reverend Christopher 'Chrimbo' McFadyen, Convener of the PC Convention (formerly known as Moderator of the General Assembly). Chrimbo, a sharp dresser, had been headhunted by image consultants as part of the Church's 'rebranding'. The Convener's job had been made into a seven-year post, and the convention itself had been transformed from a decision-making forum into a stage-managed rally for sales operatives.

In addition to Nancy Kirk and Tanya Hyde, the other members of the Council were Rev Tom 'Holy' Watters who headed up the Font Division (baptisms), Rev Alistair Husband who was in charge of the Unions Division (marriages), and Rev Sandy Heavenor who bossed the Hereafter Division (funerals). The seventh member was Ms Rita Klegg, whose job was to supervise the staff at the Livingston HQ, and to make sure that no one leaked any information to the press.

'Hello, Mr McGonigall, are you still there?'

Clarence snapped back into real time. 'Yes Nanny—I mean Nancy—I'm still here. Why do you think it's so important that I should be contactable at all times of the day and night?'

'We need to be able to keep track of all our staff,' she said.

'Ah,' said Clarence. 'It's a new form of electronic tagging for offenders.'

'We've bought a new phone for you,' Nancy went on, ignoring his irritating comments. 'I'll send one of my staff to Scunner manse tomorrow to teach you how to use it.'

'Well, here's a message from one of my staff,' said Clarence. He held out the receiver to Squeegee, who barked very loudly into the mouthpiece. There was a sound of a crashing teacup at the other end.

'Would you like to say a word to my dug?' asked Clarence.

Rev Nancy Kirk managed to recover her composure. Then she had a piece of inspiration. 'Walkies!' she shouted down the phone into Squeegee's rejoicing ear. A masterstroke. Chastened Clarence had to take her out.

It was no less a personage than the Reverend Tanya Hyde who presented herself on the doorstep of Scunner manse next morning, armed with a gleaming new mobile phone. She knew that this was going to be a challenging morning.

'I hate these things,' said Clarence. 'You can't go anywhere without that racket.'

'This phone is very easy to operate,' she told Clarence, ignoring his lament. 'When the phone goes, you press this little button, and you start speaking.'

'But it's tiny,' said Clarence. 'I'll never get this end near my mouth.'

'You don't need to,' said Tanya. 'All you do is speak. With your voice we'll probably hear you in Livingston without it.

'We've programmed your up-to-date bonus situation into the phone. This means that whenever you switch it on, a message will come up on the screen, telling you how many baptisms, weddings and funerals you are short of your bonus target.'

'Such knowledge is too wonderful for me,' said Clarence. 'It is high, I cannot attain unto it. Whither shall I go from thy spirit? Or whither shall I flee from thy presence? If I ascend up into heaven, thou art there, if I make my bed in hell, behold, thou art there.'

'What?' said Tanya.

'Nothing,' said Clarence. 'Psalm 139. Authorized Version. Before your time.'

At that very moment, Thine Be the Glory chimed out.

'What in heaven's name is that?' said Clarence.

'That's your phone,' said Tanya. 'It plays tunes. Answer it.'

'It's enough to waken the dead,' said Clarence as he pressed the button. 'Scunner Manse,' he said loudly.

'No need to shout,' said the voice on the line. Nancy Kirk.

'How did you know you would find me in the manse?' asked Clarence.

'I don't think you've grasped the concept of a mobile phone, Mr McGonigall,' said the Church's chief executive. 'You don't need to know where the person is. You just dial their number.'

There was a peal of laughter from just outside the study door. Agnes McGonigall had been listening to the tutorial, knowing that it would be pure, unmissable theatre.

'Aggie!' roared Clarence at his beloved helpmeet. 'You've been eavesdropping. Do you think you're Rita Klegg?'

Tanya Hyde glowered. Nancy Kirk spluttered. Agnes McGonigall was helpless with laughter on the floor.

'Well, I can see I'm a hit with the ladies,' said Clarence.

It was a bitterly cold day at the graveside. Why, thought Clarence, do they always choose the most exposed places for burying the dead?

The deceased, Sammy Burns, had been a bit of a reprobate, quite fond of the bottle. Clarence rather liked him.

'O, God of heaven and earth,' prayed Clarence, 'as we are mindful of thy presence in the midst of death, speak to us, in the quietness, of eternal things.'

Suddenly, Thine Be the Glory chimed out. A mobile phone. Clarence glowered at the mourners, resenting this intrusion. Surely, at a time like this...

He realised that the mourners were looking at him. It was his own mobile phone.

Clarence fished the tiny instrument out of his pocket. The chimes became louder and more insistent. What to do? He pressed the button.

'Scunner manse,' he shouted. 'I mean, Scunner graveyard.'

'Mr McGonigall? Nancy Kirk here...'

'I'm burying the dead,' roared Clarence.

A ripple of laughter went round the mourners. They knew that Sammy Burns would have enjoyed this absurd drama at his funeral. The funeral tea would be all the merrier because of it.

'I'm in the middle of a funeral,' said Clarence, 'and I'm about to bury your mobile phone.'

With that, he threw the phone into the grave, beside Sammy. Nancy was still talking.

'O death, where is thy ring?' said Jimmy McAlpine, the dead man's closest friend, and a notable wag. 'Sammy'll be able to order a round. C'mon, Clarence, you look like a dead man walking. Time for a drink.'

3. Queen Camilla and the Ghost of Jenny Geddes

Jubilate, everybody! The day of the coronation of Charles, Prince of Wales, Duke of Rothesay had at last arrived! Now, with his beloved Queen Camilla at his side, he would reign over Britain.

Not everyone was excited. Certainly not the Reverend J. Clarence McGonigall. In fact, he was distinctly underwhelmed by the whole notion.

Clarence had never even liked the opening ceremonies of the General Assembly of the old Church of Scotland. All that bowing and scraping before the Lord High Commissioner, and all that stuff about 'Your Grace' was, well, a disgrace. This was no way for a Scottish Presbyterian church to behave, he reckoned.

Sitting in his study, Clarence cast his mind back to the opening, in 1999, of Scotland's first parliament in over three hundred years, right there in the auld kirk's Assembly Hall. Clarence had been among those who had campaigned for years for a Scottish parliament.

He had sat proudly in the gallery as James MacMillan's opening fanfare struck up. He had had a lump in his throat as Sheena Wellington led the whole Assembly in singing Robert Burns' great anthem, 'A man's a man for a' that'.

Clarence couldn't help smiling as he saw the royals struggle through the verse:

> Ye see yon birkie ca'd 'a lord',
> Wha struts, an' stares, an' a' that;
> Tho' hundreds worship at his word,
> He's but a coof for a' that:
> For a' that, an' a' that,
> His ribband, star, an' a' that;
> The man o' independent mind
> He looks an' laughs at a' that.

Clarence cast his mind back to the General Assembly of 2002, held in the old Assembly Hall, before the days when it had been sold to a chain of lapdancing clubs. He groaned as he remembered the then First Minister of Scotland, Jack McConnell, looking a right tumshie as he held the Royal Purse of Scotland at an awkward angle to his body.

'What a funny way for Scotland's heid bummer to walk,' he muttered to his dog, Squeegee.

His lovable pet bounced in the air. All Squeegee had heard was the word 'walk'. There was nothing for it but to take her out.

'Clarence,' Agnes had said, two weeks before the great event, 'I need to go to Edinburgh to get a new dress.'

'A new dress, Aggie?' replied the minister. 'What on earth for?'

'The coronation,' replied Agnes coolly.

'The coronation!' said Clarence. 'I didn't know we were invited.'

'We're not,' said Agnes. 'I'll watch it on the television.'

'On the television!' exploded Clarence. 'Why do you need a new dress to watch a coronation on the television?'

'The trouble with you, Clarence,' said his wife, 'is that you have no sense of occasion.'

When the great day dawned, the sun was high in the sky. Clarence was singing as he got into his old clothes. There was no point in visiting today—everyone would be glued to the telly.

He reckoned without Agnes.

'Clarence,' she asked. 'Why are you dressed like that?'

'Because I'm going to work in the garden. It's a lovely day.'

'Have you forgotten that today is coronation day?' said Agnes, who was attired in her new red dress, red hat, and matching accessories.

'No, Aggie,' said Clarence, 'it's just that it's a waste to spend such a lovely day inside.'

'But this is a historic day. Surely you don't want to miss it?'

'I'll be able to see the edited highlights,' replied Clarence. 'They'll have them in slow motion.'

His sardonic wit made no impression on Agnes.

Clarence decided to go on to the offensive.

'Isn't it a bit odd for you to be wearing all that gear just to watch the telly in your own living room? You look more royal than the royals.'

He knew, as soon as he allowed the words to escape his lips, that he had made a grave error of judgment. His wife was ready.

'Have you forgotten what you were wearing, sitting on the couch, when Scotland were playing in the World Cup?' replied Agnes. 'Now, tell me, was that the time when they managed to draw with an Iran team in bare feet, or was it when they were humiliated by a blind team from Peru?'

Clarence winced. He knew, from experience, that there was more to come from his relentless interrogator.

'Don't I recall you wearing a Scotland strip, while you watched television pictures of Scotland players in suits, waving goodbye as they went off to win the World Cup in Argentina? And didn't you march up and down the living room, singing "We're on the march with Ally's army"? And didn't Ally's glorious army fail to win a single game?'

Squeegee wagged her tail pleadingly, as tension built in the room. Then Agnes's voice became gentler. In this domestic drama, she was playing both the hard cop and the soft cop.

'Please, Clarence,' said Agnes, 'put on your suit today, just for me. I've even got a button-hole for you. Let's make it a day to remember for the rest of our lives.'

Thus it was that a chastened Reverend J. Clarence McGonigall, semi-detached republican, found himself seated on the couch in his manse, dressed in his best suit, sporting a white carnation, watching the coronation on television, while a summer sun split the sky.

Clarence knew that the coronation would be an excruciating occasion. He even felt sympathy for the recently disestablished Church of England.

It must have been humiliating for The Episcopal Church (England), as the old C of E was now titled, to see the Mormon Church, backed by Rupert Murdoch's BSkyB, win the bid for the coronation service of King Charles.

In accordance with the government's 'Best Value' audit, all the churches had had to submit tenders in sealed envelopes. The comprehensive multi-million Mormon bid had even covered the catering franchise for the event.

Clarence could only watch the show through the cracks between his fingers. What had once been archaic theatre had now become modern, politically correct, vaudeville.

Charles solemnly promised to defend 'all faiths and creeds'.

'Oh, God,' groaned the minister, 'Royal Protector of Aromatherapy and the Flat Earth Society.'

Queen Camilla was then presented with a copy of the Book of Mormon.

'Well, I suppose polygamy was more honest,' muttered Clarence.

Sky television's live, interactive coverage gave viewers the option of watching the service from a variety of angles. They also had the opportunity to vote on the costumes worn by Queen Camilla and the rest of the royals. One of those sending in a correct entry would win an Aston Martin open-topped sports car. Aggie pressed the voting button on the remote control with great enthusiasm.

As the American Mormon bishop placed the crown on the head of King Charles, a choir sang a religious chorus of unspeakable banality. That was bad enough, but what came next tipped the demented Clarence McGonigall over the edge.

In the middle of the prayers for the King and Queen, uttered by a black American New Age guru with a wooden leg, the results of the fashion poll were flashed up on the screen.

This was a step too far.

The Reverend J. Clarence McGonigall stood up, lifted a nearby wooden stool, and hurled it at the television screen.

On earth, Mrs Agnes McGonigall fainted. In heaven, Jenny Geddes clapped her hands.

The hammering at the manse door was insistent. Neighbours wanted to know what was going on. They found their minister semi-coherent, pouring brandy down the throat of the somewhat overdressed lady of the manse.

'Aggie will be fine in a minute,' said Clarence. 'Go home and prepare for democracy.'

The television was still blaring away, but there was no picture. Glass lay all over the living room floor.

In the middle of the mayhem, the phone went. A breezy executive from Sky Television gave Clarence the news that Aggie had won the open-topped sports car. They would like the happy couple to pose in front of a big poster of King Charles and Queen Camilla.

The neighbours went home to prepare drinks.

Agnes was right. They would remember this historic day for the rest of their lives.

4. Great Balls of Fire!

A great sense of weariness came over the Reverend J. Clarence McGonigall as he contemplated the command to attend a bonding session for ministers. Things had become intolerable since the privatisation of the Church of Scotland—now called The Presbyterian Church (Scotland).

It was in the year 2008 that consultants had decided, after extensive and costly market research, that The Presbyterian Church (Scotland) had an image problem. It was far too gloomy and negative. A new logo was designed with the slogan 'Smile with Jesus!', accompanied by a rotund Mr Happy figure.

The Kirk's old headquarters at 121 George Street, Edinburgh had been sold to Kentucky Fried Chicken, and custom-built premises had been erected at an industrial estate in Livingston. Clarence's query at the General Assembly as to whether the architect had been the same as the one who had designed Nissen huts during the war had not gone down well.

The sale of the Assembly Hall on the Mound to a national chain of lapdance clubs—Clarence hadn't a clue what lapdancing was all about, but he sensed that John Knox wouldn't have approved—raised a substantial sum, which was used to fund the appointment of Regional Growth Directors.

These perpetually cheery young zealots, who had been given the remit of 'modernizing' the Church's mission, had all been sent to America for training.

'Religious snake-oil salesmen,' Clarence had muttered.

The bonding sessions, the compulsory invitation informed him, would be held up and down the country—one in every SuperPresbytery, in fact. Any minister who failed to attend would lose his Easter bonus, even if he had met all his yearly targets.

'Dress will be informal,' instructed the letter. 'The object of the overnight event is to promote team-building, so that we can focus more clearly on our objectives.'

'Haud me back,' said Clarence to his dog, Squeegee, who responded by wagging her tail.

'Guess what, Aggie,' he shouted to his beloved helpmeet. 'I've to go on a bonding course with members of the SuperPresbytery!'

'Bondage course? With the Presbytery?' queried Agnes, putting her head in the study. 'Are you sure? Is that not illegal?'

'Bonding,' reiterated her husband. 'Not only is it not illegal, it's compulsory.'

'Is it compulsory for me to come too?' asked Agnes.

'No, Aggie. You're spared,' replied her husband.

Mineral water and orange juice were served with dinner at the Church's training centre. Clarence had anticipated that. His hipflask was in his back pocket.

'Well, this is a jolly occasion,' he muttered to his pal, Gavin McAllister.

'Don't speak too loud,' grinned Gavin. 'It's old unreconstructed duffers like you that they're trying to re-educate. You might get singled out for one of the games.'

'Games?' said Clarence. 'What games?'

'Just you wait,' said Gavin.

Some of the ministers were a little self-conscious in their informal gear. Two in their fifties had squeezed themselves into jeans that had accommodated them fairly easily some years ago, but failed to do so now.

The meal was followed by the singing of a banal chorus which made Clarence wince. Then one of the Regional Growth Directors stood up to give a pep talk.

'The Church is operating in a very difficult market today,' said the Rev Arthur—'call me "Art"'—Christopher.

'If we are to enlarge our customer base,' said Art, 'we need to be sure what our product is, and define it clearly. Then we need to use the best modern technology in order to sell our product. Our product is, of course, God.'

Clarence snorted. He had to speak.

'So does our progress make commercial travellers of us all, and take away the primeval joy in sun, in wind, in divine idleness?' he said, in a voice loud enough to be heard by everyone.

Silence fell upon the room.

'What do you mean by that?' asked Art.

Clarence rose to his feet.

'That is a quote from R. B. Cunninghame Graham, one of the wisest Scots ever to have lived,' he said. 'It is very apposite, don't you think?'

The anarchic Cunninghame Graham was one of Clarence McGonigall's heroes. Clarence knew what the great man would have made of all of this talk about religious 'product'.

'It might have been wisdom in the twentieth century, but not for today,' retorted Art with a forced smile. 'The wisdom for the twenty-first century is that what we focus on is what we get. And if we focus on divine idleness, we may end up out of a job.'

'Maybe the job of the Church is to challenge today's wisdom,' came back Clarence. 'God is not a product to be sold, but a life to be lived.'

'Sit down, Clarence,' whispered Gavin. 'Remember your bonus.'

'If we have faith,' went on Art, determined to get back on track, 'we can achieve anything. The most successful entrepreneurs of the ages have reduced their message to utter simplicity, in such a way that it can go into an advertising jingle. Then they have conquered the world. We can do the same. That is the message of Jesus. Focus on the product, and believe with all your might. Do that, and you will be successful.'

'I think someone should crucify Mr Happy,' said Clarence, in a clearly audible aside.

Silence reigned.

Everyone was asked to go outside. In the grounds of the centre was a line of burning coals. Art told them they were going to do a firewalk. They were instructed to take off their shoes and socks.

The Presbytery Clerk was first to remove the trainers which he had borrowed from his son. (If the letter said 'informal', then informal it would have to be.)

'I'm going to prove that this faith business works,' said Art. 'We've done this in several Presbyteries, and no one has been hurt.'

'So far,' muttered Clarence. 'It's a while since we had a Presbyterian burning.'

'It's all about belief,' Art ploughed on. 'You can run across these red-hot coals without burning your feet. When you do it, you'll feel great. You'll feel empowered. You'll be ready to take on the world.'

Jonathan Thomson, the other Regional Growth Director, demonstrated it. He walked quickly across the coals, whooping as he went.

'Any volunteers?' asked Art.

The Presbytery Clerk stepped forward. Ever since he had been put in charge of a SuperPresbytery, he felt he had to show leadership.

He started hesitantly, then ran quickly across the coals. At the end of the path, he jumped in the air with delight, and exultantly did 'high fives' with Art.

'Who's next?' shouted Art.

Clarence's hour had come. He took a swig from his hip flask, then stepped forward.

He could feel his heart thumping. Could he do it? He would soon find out. Aggie would never believe this.

Suddenly, he turned towards the firewalk, began to run, then hurtled himself through the air, roaring 'Great balls of fire!'

One step, two steps, and he was there. Applause broke out.

'I don't know what's in that hipflask,' muttered Gavin, 'but I want some.'

Art stood at the starting-point, staring. He wanted to do the firewalk more stylishly than that old irritant who had knocked him off his stride earlier in the evening. It was people like him who were obstacles to change in the church.

Art had done this several times before. There was nothing to worry about.

Was there?

His mouth felt a little dry as he approached the fire walk. Then he sprang on to the burning flames.

A fearful scream rent the air. Aaaaaaaaaaaargh!

Art fell on to the ground, and lay there crumpled, his feet blistered.

Clarence rushed forward, pulling the hipflask out of his pocket. Then he poured the amber liquid on to Art's feet, and rubbed them.

'Twelve year old single malt,' said Clarence. 'Good for the sole.'

'How did it go?' asked Agnes.

'Fine, Aggie,' said Clarence. 'We bonded well, and I feel great. To think I'd said I'd rather run along hot coals in my bare feet than go to one of these events.'

5. Ann Widdecombe Beggars Belief

Whenever he saw the prime minister on television, the Reverend J. Clarence McGonigall winced. Ann Widdecombe could set his teeth on edge like no one else. Now she was addressing the nation.

'In order to protect this country from the influx of illegal immigrants,' she said, 'the government is planning to introduce a system of identity cards. Every citizen will be expected to carry one. Only those who have been guilty of wrongdoing need fear the new arrangements.'

Clarence groaned. He had been here before, many times. He remembered how, in 2002, the Labour Home secretary, David Blunkett, had introduced a similar proposal. After massive public protests, the then prime minister, Tony Blair, ever the populist, had ensured that the proposal had been quietly withdrawn.

Now it was becoming law. The cavernous John Redmond was on screen, explaining how the new system would work.

'Each identity card will have a small microchip,' said the Home Secretary. 'It will contain the bearer's details, employment records, health records and benefit entitlements. It will have a special iris print, which will make it impossible to forge. This little card will ensure the liberty of every citizen.'

Clarence groaned again.

'George Orwell, where are you, now that we need you,' he muttered. 'This is newspeak, weasel talk.'

His dog, Squeegee, bounced high in the air. She thought she had heard the word 'walk'. He had to take her out.

Clarence McGonigall had never put much trust in political parties. He inclined towards Scottish nationalism with a social conscience, but he believed too much in original sin to be enchanted by any of the political utopias on offer.

He had, though, entertained high hopes of Tony Blair. After his second landslide victory in 2001, Blair had had the opportunity to make radical political changes, but he had opted for caution and popularity. He wanted to hold on to power.

His defeat in the euro referendum, followed by opinion polls which showed that Labour's popularity was in terminal decline, pushed Blair to resign and move to the House of Lords. Ann Widdecombe, who had become something of a cult figure in the 'family values' movement and who had outshone the lacklustre Iain Duncan Smith in the campaign against the single currency, had become leader of the Conservatives after a bloody coup.

Gordon Brown's defeat in 2005 had been part of a swing to the radical Right throughout Europe. The British Tory campaign promise of reducing income tax to 13p in the pound had been a vote-winner.

Four years on, the political landscape of Britain had changed drastically.

'I feel like an alien in my own country, Aggie,' Clarence said to his wife of forty years. 'Now we've got to have identity cards. There are cameras everywhere in the streets. Big Brother is watching you.'

'Maybe you should be watching Big Brother,' joked Agnes, referring to the cult television programme which had held the nation in thrall for more than a decade.

'When that day comes,' replied Clarence, 'you'll know it's time to take me out and shoot me.'

What troubled Clarence deeply nowadays was the silent, inexorable disintegration of any sense of shared values. As a sensitive and caring man, he could feel within his being the turning of people away from each other, a retreat into private, individual concerns.

The large numbers of unemployed, the homelessness, and the growing drug dependency had given the country a shadowy and ominous feel. Many people were wealthy, especially since the tax-cutting budgets, but most seemed to be under continual stress at work. Their homes were not just their castles, but fortresses.

It was as if people had become blinded, and did not even know the extent of their loss.

The privatized spirituality of Scotland's churches distressed Clarence. The Presbyterian Church (Scotland) had abolished the Church and Nation Committee of the old Church of Scotland. It was, said its ascendant critics, nothing but a posturing left-wing clique which undermined the gospel.

'We'll be having show trials next,' Clarence had told a bewildered Squeegee.

The new leaders of the Presbyterian Church insisted that Christianity had nothing to do with politics. It was about, apparently, cultivating the individual soul. It also had to do with 'possibility thinking', with getting on in the world.

The tone had been set by the Reverend Christopher McFadyen. Bedecked in open-necked silk shirt, jewellery, designer jeans and glittering cross, the Convener of the PC Convention provided words of assurance.

'The person who becomes converted to Christ,' he crooned soothingly in a mid-Atlantic accent as an electronic organ played softly in the background, 'had better get ready to move to a better job and a better house. Because with God, all things are possible.'

'How about murder?' Clarence had muttered to his friend, Gavin McAllister. 'It would certainly liven up this ghastly religious sales conference.'

Disapproving heads turned.

'Wheest,' said Gavin, sucking a pan drop, 'you'll have your bonuses cut off.'

When the confrontation came, it was in circumstances no one could have expected. The prime minister was making a swing through Scotland, as part of the general election campaign. The polls predicted confidently that she would win a second term with a landslide majority.

Menteith was Conservative country. Ann Widdecombe was in buoyant form on her walkabout.

'We will make even more tax cuts,' she promised, to ecstatic applause from bystanders. 'We will stop all subsidies to the feckless. We will allow business to flourish, with fewer handicaps. We will make this a land which honours the divine law. We will clear the beggars from the streets.'

'How dare you!' cried one of the street beggars, standing up suddenly. The television cameras turned on him. This was not in the script.

'How dare you come to the birthplace of Robert Cunninghame Graham and spout this reactionary nonsense,' the man cried. The crowds closed in, to watch this piece of street theatre.

'Cunninghame Graham fought all his life against the things you are doing,' the man shouted in a loud voice.

Taking a piece of paper from his pocket, he went on, 'Here is what he said: "Day by day the working classes, owing to the pressure of laws facetiously called

economic and divine, are sinking into a worse condition. Is there anything divine in the law which allows one man to create a royalty or a robbery on the minerals he did not create, or in the system that allows one man to build up a colossal fortune by rendering half of his fellow countrymen little better than slaves? I see nothing more than pure devil's work in that."

'Our Scottish church may be neutered,' the man went on, 'but we have a tradition here of Christian protest against those rulers who fail in their duty in defend the poor.'

With one sudden movement, the beggar stepped forward, and pushed a custard pie into the face of the astonished prime minister. The security men stepped in quickly, and took the man away.

Agnes McGonigall was lying in a reverie on the couch in Scunner manse when the national news came on the television. She saw the prime minister in the streets of Menteith. She heard the despairing cry of the beggar.

When the camera turned upon him, Agnes sat up, bolt upright.

'Clarence!' she shouted. 'It's Clarence! Dressed as a beggar! And that's the custard pie I bought this morning!'

In court, the Reverend J. Clarence McGonigall was found guilty of breach of the peace. Asked if he had anything to say, he replied simply that Christian voices had to be raised on behalf of the poor and the underprivileged, especially at the birthplace of the anarchic aristocrat, Sir Robert Cunninghame Graham.

He quoted Graham: 'It may be that all of us are kings born blind, and that the guiding star is shining brightly in the sky, whilst we sit sightless, with our dim orbits fixed upon the mud.'

The court heard a letter from the Rev Christopher McFadyen, Convener of the Convention of the Presbyterian Church (Scotland), apologizing for the discourteous behaviour of one of the Church's ministers, and assuring the court that he would be disciplined.

Clarence smiled wrily. 'Jesus wept,' was all he said.

Aggie paid the fine.

6. The Re-formation of the Winter Man

'Aggie!' roared the Reverend J. Clarence McGonigall. 'Aggie, come right away! I've got shocking news!'

When Agnes McGonigall ran into the study, she saw her husband holding up a letter. She saw that he was trembling. Was he about to have a heart attack?

'What's the matter, Clarence?' she asked her husband, anxiously. 'Is it bad news? Have your bonuses been stopped?'

'No, it's much worse than that,' said Clarence. 'I can hardly take it in.'

'What does it say?' said Agnes. 'Read it to me. I think I better sit down.'

'Dear Mr McGonigall,' read Clarence.

'Never mind all that,' said Agnes. 'Just tell me the worst.'

'Dear Mr McGonigall,' Clarence continued, 'As you know, the image of the Presbyterian Church (Scotland) is crucial in its efforts to widen market share. The Church has to present a positive, attractive image to the world.

'Since ministers are the Church's frontline amb-assadors, attention is being paid to individual clergy.

Our image consultants have advised us that some of our ministers are giving a bad impression of the Church. You are considered to be in need of a makeover.'

Agnes McGonigall snorted with laughter. Clarence had the feeling that he was about to be denied yet again the sympathy that should be afforded by a loyal spouse.

'Consequently,' Clarence continued reading, 'you will be visited by a member of staff from Livingston, who will be authorised to implement changes to your personal appearance. The costs of the makeover will be borne entirely by the Presbyterian Church (Scotland). We confidently expect your co-operation in this matter.'

By this time, Agnes was overcome with laughter. Her husband had never paid the slightest attention to fashion, and the notion of him having a makeover was almost too delicious to be true.

'What would they want to change about my appearance anyway?' asked Clarence, plaintively.

'Where would you like me to begin?' asked Agnes.

The letter was signed by the Reverend Nancy Kirk, the Presbyterian Church (Scotland)'s chief executive. Clarence dialled the number immediately.

'Nanny, I mean Nancy, this is a ridiculous letter,' spluttered Clarence. 'What a waste of the Church's money!'

'I was expecting this call, Mr McGonigall,' said the chief executive. 'This policy has been approved by the Council of Seven...'

'I might have known the Star Chamber was involved,' interrupted Clarence. 'Can you imagine some self-important committee telling John Knox to come in and have his beard trimmed in case Mary Queen of Scots was offended?'

'John Knox could have done with an image consultant,' said Nancy. 'He was an uncouth, foul-mouthed fanatic who should have had a proper training in manners and diplomacy, as well as having his beard removed.'

'What if I refuse to co-operate?' retorted the furious minister.

'Your bonuses will be cut off,' said Nancy Kirk, curtly.

Agnes, who had been eavesdropping on the phone in the living room, burst out, 'You must do it, Clarence. We need a new television!'

'Aggie! How dare you listen in! Do you think you are Rita Klegg?' shouted a mortified Clarence.

'Mr McGonigall,' went on Nancy, 'I and a consultant will present ourselves at Scunner manse on Monday at 11am. Your makeover will begin then.'

'This is a ridiculous waste of money,' spluttered Clarence. 'I am due to retire soon. What's the point of changing my appearance at this stage?'

'Because you represent a challenge to us,' responded the chief executive. 'If we can change you, we can change anyone.'

The doorbell rang at 11am precisely. Nancy Kirk introduced the youthful image consultant, Julian Snodgrass, and his glamorous assistant, Miranda Messenger. Squeegee, sensing danger to her master, snarled at them.

'Control your dog, please, Mr McGonigall,' ordered Nancy, as Clarence ushered them into the study. 'I suggest you keep it out of the room, as we don't wish to be covered with dog hairs.'

'No, we can't have modern servants of the Lord with dog hairs on them,' replied Clarence. 'When Jesus was being crucified, his beautician picked the dog hairs off his loincloth. You can tell, because you don't see dog hairs in any of the great paintings of the crucifixion.'

'I can see that you are going to be your usual truculent self, Mr McGonigall,' said Nancy. 'Your makeover is long overdue. Has there been a blizzard in Scunner this morning, or is that dandruff on your shoulders?'

Clarence, dressed in his usual crumpled suit and dog collar, glowered. He stood uneasily, as Julian and his assistant circled him, taking notes.

'You are a winter person, Mr McGonigall,' said Julian. 'You are wearing the wrong colours. You need bright, striking shades to counterbalance your complexion and your eyes. If you want to appeal to the modern generation, you need to wear more modern, casual clothes. Your hair must be redone completely. We can attend to that now, before we take you to buy a new outfit.'

'Tell me, what do you know about Christianity?'
Clarence inquired.

'I think it's a bit old fashioned myself,' said Julian. 'I
believe in spirituality. I do spiritual dance at weekend
workshops.'

'I think you're just the man to lead our next Super-
Presbytery training session,' said Clarence.

Miranda opened up the big box she had brought.
There were scissors, lotions, dyes, and a hairdryer. The
transformation began with a shampoo and styling.

'You need a more daring, modern style, Mr
McGonigall,' simpered Miranda as she began
removing most of his hair. Soon, there was only a
strip of hair running down the centre of the minister's
head.

'Your hair is white,' said Miranda. 'That makes you
look too old. You need something more striking.'

She took a spray from her box, and within seconds the strip of hair was red. Nancy Kirk clapped her hands with delight. 'Now we must get you some clothes,' she said.

The boutique in Inverness blared out young people's music. To say that the Reverend J. Clarence McGonigall felt out of place would be an understatement of very high proportions.

After a conversation with Julian Snodgrass, the shop assistant came forward with a pair of drainpipe tight cream trousers. The look, which had been the height of fashion in the 1950s, was back in vogue. A brown suede jacket with big shoulders was next, followed by a pair of tapered, winklepicker shoes, of the type which Clarence had worn as a youth. A cream, open-necked shirt completed the outfit, before the bewildered minister was wheeled into a jeweller's shop. There, a big, gold cross was hung around his neck.

'Now we have you,' said Nancy. 'At last, you are a proper ambassador for the Presbyterian Church in the year 2009.'

The Reverend Nancy Kirk sat on her couch, watching the evening news on television. She was on her fourth glass of champagne to celebrate the reformation and repackaging of Clarence McGonigall, the bane of her existence. How she would enjoy telling the staff at Livingston about her triumph!

'...And finally, a tale of charity and compassion to touch the heartstrings,' said the TV announcer. 'We bring you a story about a person who lives out what he believes in.'

The camera moved to a man wearing a cream shirt and drainpipe trousers, a brown suede jacket and winklepicker shoes. Round his neck was a sparkling gold cross.

'I've been on hard times,' he told the TV interviewer. 'I had hardly a decent shirt for my back, so I went to seek help from a good man. After I'd told him my story, he asked me to wait for a minute. When he came back, he offered me the fine clothes he had been wearing. I've never met Christianity in action like this before. I'm so impressed that I've decided to join the Church.'

The camera switched to the Reverend Clarence McGonigall, dressed in his familiar scruffy suit. The only unusual thing was that he wore a hat.

'It was nothing,' said Clarence, shyly. Then he looked straight into the camera. 'You have to make sacrifices sometimes, if you want to be an ambassador for the church in the year 2009.' He spoke these words slowly and deliberately, with the merest hint of a smile.

Nancy Kirk fell off her couch, rolled over, and drummed her legs on the floor. 'Murder!' screamed the normally prim, but now slightly inebriated, chief executive of the Presbyterian Church (Scotland). 'Who shall rid me of this troublesome priest?'

7. Tear up a Questionnaire for Jesus

The busy people at church headquarters were always coming up with new ideas. Documents setting out newer and dafter targets flooded in upon Clarence, adding to the overwhelming weariness he was experiencing. He felt like the dead horse which could not be flogged any more.

It was a source of frustration to the church authorities that the Reverend J. Clarence McGonigall had resolutely refused to buy a computer. In this year of Our Lord, 2009, he was probably the only minister in the Presbyterian Church (Scotland) without one. Frustrated officials at the church's headquarters in Livingston had whined and pleaded, arguing that they would be able to get messages faster to him.

That was precisely why Clarence didn't want one. Enough junk reached him by post without the stuff flooding through the ether as well. Immediate replies would be requested, nay demanded.

When letters came via the postman, you could stick them in a file, or on the floor, or even in the fire. Usually, no great harm would come of this strategy. Occasionally there would be irate phone calls from

Livingston, but by and large the flurry of mail was 'sound and fury signifying nothing'.

He had long since ignored questionnaires. He agreed with one of his favourite poets, W. H. Auden:

> Thou shalt not answer questionnaires
> Nor quizzes upon world affairs
> Nor with compliance
> Take any test. Thou shalt not sit
> With statisticians, nor commit
> A social science.

He well remembered one huge survey from someone calling himself modestly 'the Liaison Officer for National Renewal'. After looking at the first question on page one of the wretched fifteen-page document— 'What are the likes and dislikes of your community?' —he had felt like lying down in a darkened room for a while. Instead, he quickly answered under 'likes': 'Cheese and onion crisps', and 'dislikes': 'questionnaires'. He had then signed the form, and put it in the post.

Three years on, he had not heard a word in response. Was there some big missionary map at Livingston HQ with 'Cheese and onion crisps' written above the parish of Inversnecky North, linked with Scunner South, linked with Trachle (Continuing), linked with Havers Memorial?

It depressed Clarence that so many of his ministerial colleagues seemed to be slaves to the computer. Clarence had always held to the view that the ministry of word and sacrament was primarily about preaching, prayer and pastoral work. Now the modern minister was a deskbound functionary, staring at a screen, typing meaningless reports.

Clarence winced when younger clerics talked about working in their 'office'. They had fallen for the seductive lie that high-tech technology inevitably brought freedom, and that machines would eventually do away with paperwork. What had actually happened was that the volume of the slurry had increased exponentially with the rise and rise of electronic technology.

Not only were files bulging with paper just in case a bug invaded the wretched computer, but bureaucracy was running amok. Clarence agreed with the words of Pierre Gallois, 'If you put tomfoolery into a computer, nothing comes out but tomfoolery. But this tomfoolery, having passed through a very expensive machine, is somehow ennobled and no one dares criticise it.'

Clarence, who defiantly founded The Friends of Canute (Tear up a Questionnaire for Jesus section), was also fond of quoting Nicholas I: 'I do not rule Russia, ten thousand clerks do'.

As he looked around his book-lined study, Clarence felt like a dinosaur. He pulled out *The Technological Society* by one of his favourite authors, Jacques Ellul.

'When technique enters into every area of life, including the human,' wrote Ellul, 'it ceases to be external to man and becomes his very substance.'

Clarence sighed as he looked at the pile of mail. 'This is enough to give one the boak,' he muttered to his dog.

Squeegee jumped in the air. She was sure her master had said the magic word, 'walk'. She would have to go out now. The paperwork could wait...

When he got round to opening the pile, there were several letters with the familiar migraine-inducing yellow 'Smile with Jesus' logo. Church headquarters calling.

One letter nearly induced a stroke.

'Dear Mr McGonigall, as speedy communications are of the essence of modern ministry, it has been decided that all clergypersons should be computerised. Since you have previously refused to buy a computer, we have decided to give you one free of charge. We will send someone to install your computer and teach you how to use it.

'We are aware of past truculence on your part. Should you refuse to co-operate, you will lose your Easter bonuses.'

'Aggie,' he roared through to his beloved helpmeet, 'I've got disastrous news. I've to get a computer.'

Agnes came running through, screaming with laughter.

'A computer!' she cried. 'In Scunner manse! This event must be mentioned in the book of Revelation!'

'This isn't funny, Aggie,' said Clarence, sternly.

'You don't think so?' said Agnes, doubled up with mirth.

'They say that if I refuse, they'll cut off my Easter bonuses.'

The smile froze on his wife's face.

'You'll have to have the computer, then.'

The young man who came from the Livingston headquarters to Scunner manse realised fairly soon that he was on to a loser. He quickly had the new computer up and running, but the brain of its intended operator did not appear to be functioning nearly as well as the machine.

Five minutes into the spiel about how to operate the equipment, Clarence interrupted.

'You know,' he said, 'I haven't understood a single word you have said. You'll need to speak to me as if you are talking to a child.'

'That's what I've been doing,' said the young man.

'Then pretend I'm a foetus,' said Clarence.

Agnes came in with tea, quivering with laughter. As she exited from the study, a great peal of laughter broke through her dam of suppression and echoed through the manse.

Clarence overheard Agnes on the phone to her friend, Jessie. He heard her sob through hysterical laughter, 'Pretend I'm a foetus.'

He expected a bit more sympathy from the lady of the manse.

The young man, realising he was in bewildering and even dangerous territory, carried on with the tutorial, using exaggerated gestures and words of one syllable. He sounded like the interpreter of a long-lost language.

Eventually, Clarence managed to put together one simple document.

The young man was as ecstatic as if he had just climbed Everest.

'Yes!' he cried, punching the air, 'Yes!'

Next day, Clarence decided to prepare Sunday's service on the new machine. Using one finger, he laboriously typed out the whole service. It took him four hours. He felt almost proud of his new skills.

He even phoned his friend, Gavin McAllister, who had been computer-literate for years.

'I knew you'd eventually be sent to a re-education camp,' said Gavin. 'You're lucky they didn't threaten to cut off more than your bonuses. Anyway, Clarence, welcome to the twentieth century—even if the rest of us are living in the twenty-first.'

Clarence felt exhilarated. That is, until he returned to the screen. Nothing.

He tried switching on some knobs and switching off others. Still nothing. He was frantic.

Hell hath no fury like a minister whose Sunday service hath vanished down some black hole. The Reverend J. Clarence McGonigall, MA, BD, shouted, ranted, and uttered words which ministers shouldn't say, even on their day off.

He tried praying to the computer, imploring it to put the words back on the screen. He even attempted to blackmail the machine, promising to repent of his anti-technological sins, but it simply sat there, blankly, refusing to surrender its lost treasures.

Then the minister completely lost it. He threw books at the computer, then whipped it with Squeegee's lead. Exhausted, he lay down on the floor in front of the computer, curled up, yes, like a foetus. Squeegee, concerned, licked her master's face.

This was the piteous sight which greeted Mrs Agnes McGonigall when she returned from shopping.

'Oh Clarence, I don't think you've mastered this new technology business,' she said. 'I think the President of the Friends of Canute needs a stiff brandy.'

'Aye, Aggie,' said Clarence, opening one eye, 'and cheese and onion crisps.'

8. The Famous Grouse Meets the Hovis Communion

'Oh no, oh no, oh no!' screamed the Reverend J. Clarence McGonigall, frightening his dog, Squeegee. 'How much more can one human being take? This is enough to drive anyone to drink!'

Agnes, his beloved helpmeet, came running into the study.

'What's the matter, Clarence?' She noticed that he was holding a letter. 'Is it some terrible news?'

'Yes,' replied her husband. 'I've got to go to another SuperPresbytery training course.'

'Can you not tell them you've got a funeral?' asked Agnes.

'No, Aggie, it's in a month's time. How can I tell them that somebody's going to die in a month, and that they've booked their funeral? Mission Control in Livingston wouldn't believe me. Nor would the SuperPresbytery. They haven't believed any of my previous excuses.'

'I'm not surprised,' said Agnes. 'Remember the time you sent a sick note from your mother? And she had been dead for thirty years!'

'That was a joke, Aggie. It's called post-modern irony. The Livingston Lubyanka doesn't go in for irony. No, I'll have to go. Nothing else for it, unless I pretend to be dead.'

'You do a pretty good imitation sometimes,' retorted his dearly beloved, 'especially in front of the telly at night.'

'Thanks, Aggie,' said Clarence, 'Just remember that even the great prophets were mocked.'

Squeegee bounced in the air. She was sure she'd heard 'walk'. She would have to be taken out.

When he returned, Clarence looked again at the letter, which said that the forthcoming training event was part of a national series on marketing.

'Dear colleague,' it read, 'in the year 2009 our Church must be ever ready to consolidate and improve its market share. The Presbyterian Church (Scotland) is a unique brand; we need now to extend into new markets, and to improve our image.

'We can do this by associating our name with successful products, while at the same time increasing our national and local revenues by means of sponsorship. This is a much more sophisticated method of raising funds than organising jumble sales, bakery stalls and used clothes shops.

'At this exciting training event, our experts will tell you how to create a brand image in your community, and give you advice as to how to achieve local sponsorship.

'At national headquarters, we are playing our part. I am proud to inform you that the Presbyterian Church (Scotland) has completed a sponsorship deal with Hovis, the bread manufacturers. It will be worth £1 million to the Church over the next three years. In all future publicity material, would you please refer to communion as "The Hovis Communion".'

'The Hovis Communion!' chortled Clarence. 'This is a brilliant spoof! I'll bet it's Gavin McAllister winding me up!'

'No,' said Gavin when Clarence phoned him. 'I can assure you it's genuine. I've got a letter as well. You'll just have to move with the times, you old reactionary! That's why they're sending you to all these re-education camps! From now on, pal, it's the Hovis Communion.'

'You couldn't make this stuff up,' said Clarence.

'The Church is operating in a very difficult market at the end of the first decade of the twenty-first century,' said the Rev Arthur—'call me "Art"'—Christopher. 'In order to compete, we must be much more aggressive in our marketing strategy. Our brand image must be much more clearly defined. All negativity must be banished. The public must be presented with an image of the Church which is positive, happy and successful at all times.'

'Just as well Jesus was elected Rotarian of the Year,' interjected Clarence.

Art glowered. 'We've had trouble with you before,' he said.

Gavin dug Clarence in the ribs. 'Your bonuses,' he reminded him.

'Jesus wasn't Mr Happy,' Clarence charged on, disregarding his friend's admonition. 'He told people to take up their cross and follow him. He didn't say "always look on the bright side of life", and "every cloud has a silver lining".

'He told Herod he was a fox, and he threw the moneychangers out of the temple. He was crucified as an outlaw on the town garbage heap. And he wouldn't have had any time for all this superficial rubbish.'

An uneasy silence fell upon the room. There was much shuffling of feet, and gazing at the ceiling.

Then Clarence continued: 'Another thing Jesus didn't say was "I am the Hovis of life". We've moved from Holy Communion to the Hovis Communion, and we call that progress? Why didn't we do a deal with Oddbins as well, and call it the "Hovis and Beaujolais Communion"?'

At this point the Reverend Arthur Christopher completely lost it.

'It's people like you who are holding back the modern message of the Church,' he shouted at Clarence, veins standing out from his temple. 'We are doing our best to create a positive brand image, and you go and spoil it! How can the Church present a united front if people like you refuse to toe the line?'

'Well, well,' said Clarence. 'It seems that Mr Happy has become Mr Angry. I think I like you better when you're passionate.'

It was Sponsorship Sunday. Every congregation in the land was commanded to display the fruits of their efforts. Several churches had already been featured in the national press. A Prudential Insurance banner hung from the spire of St Giles Cathedral. A church in Ibrox had its exterior painted blue and white. The Canongate Kirk had a huge picture of King Charles and Queen Camilla.

But what of the parish of Inversnecky North, linked with Scunner South, linked with Trachle (Continuing), linked with Havers Memorial? There was no visible, outward sign of sponsorship. If the Reverend J. Clarence McGonigall had anything planned, he was revealing nothing.

'It will be a surprise,' he told *The Inversnecky Courier*. 'As a law-abiding, on-message minister of the Presbyterian Church (Scotland), I will, of course, be participating fully in this historic, national event. But I don't want to reveal anything.'

These enigmatic remarks had simply fuelled nervous speculation in the congregation. Scunner Church was packed full of curious people, many of whom rarely came to church despite their affection for their unpredictable parish minister. There was a buzz about the place.

There were no banners inside, no signs of sponsorship —not even for Scunner's famous Oatcakes. If Clarence

was participating in Sponsorship Sunday, he had a strange way of showing it.

There was a hush as the beadle, Sandy McPherson, entered, carrying the Bible. A smile played about his lips. Clarence followed him down the aisle in his familiar, shuffling gait.

Suddenly there was a gasp, followed by a burst of laughter, from people at the rear of the kirk. On the back of their minister's gown was a huge number 9. Above it was printed the name 'Roddy Grant', the 41-year-old, pot-bellied footballer who was still Brechin City's number-one striker after twelve years with the club.

Clarence wasn't the only one wearing a dog collar. He was followed by Squeegee, who had a collar around her neck, with the words 'Pal Meat for Happy Dogs' printed on it. She had been bewildered when her master had whispered 'walkies', and the next thing she knew was that she was walking down the aisle of the kirk.

Another gasp from the congregation came when Clarence turned round, smiling. There, ironed on to the front of his cassock, were the words 'The Famous Grouse'.

Personal sponsorship from a Scottish whisky firm was not quite what the organisers had in mind.

After the first hymn, Clarence delighted the children at the front by giving Squeegee a spoonful of the contents of a Pal dogmeat tin. Then he asked the youngsters if they would like to try some. They recoiled, as did the adult members of the congregation who were given a similar invitation.

Then Clarence ate a spoonful himself.

'Chocolate mousse,' he revealed. 'Don't believe the packaging. It's what's inside that counts.'

When Squeegee suddenly woofed for more, her master turned to the congregation, and observed, 'You know, we're all barking.'

Back at Scunner manse, Clarence asked, 'What did you think of that, Aggie?'

'Never a truer word, Clarence,' she replied. 'You're the most famous grouse in Scotland!'

'Remember,' said Clarence, 'I told you that the great prophets were mocked.'

Squeegee bounced again, then brought her lead. It had been a good day for her.

9. Strikes for us now the Hour of Grace

Sitting in the study at Scunner manse, the Reverend J. Clarence McGonigall was a troubled man. He was due to be Santa Claus at the local nursery school party in half an hour and his back was sore, but that was not what was bothering him. It was a deeper malaise, something which gnawed at his very core.

His ruminations were interrupted by the arrival of the morning mail. Squeegee's barking alerted him to the arrival of the postman. On Christmas Eve, the mail was, understandably, later than usual.

Clarence went through the cards listlessly, putting them in a pile for Agnes to look at when she returned from the shops. The card he was hoping for wasn't there. Not this Christmas, in the year of Our Lord, 2009. Nor the one before that. No, not for more years than he cared to remember.

The absence was Clarence's private wound. It hurt him.

With a sigh, the minister got up, put on his coat, and walked through the falling snow to the nursery. The Salvation Army band was playing carols at the shops near the school. Hardy bystanders joined in the singing:

> In the bleak midwinter
> Frosty winds made moan,
> Earth stood hard as iron,
> Water, like a stone.
> Snow had fallen, snow on snow,
> Snow on snow,
> In the bleak midwinter,
> Long ago.

The bleak midwinter wasn't so long ago. In fact, it was happening in the heart of the Reverend J. Clarence McGonigall.

The children cheered him up. They always did. Their faces were shining as Santa came into the room, carrying the anticipated black plastic bag. As he came forward, the singing began:

> Jingle bells, jingle bells,
> Jingle all the way.
> Oh what fun it is to ride
> On a one horse open sleigh!

Such rituals, thought Clarence, were like liturgies. They brought transcendent longings to earth. Clarence never failed to notice how much the adults enjoyed singing such unprepossessing words as much as the innocent children did. The parents and grandparents in the room, bruised by life's struggles, were, as always, both wistful and hopeful. They felt momentarily free to set down the burdens of their pasts, while they looked at their own futures in the shape of little children singing about jingling bells, while a man in a red coat and a fake white beard cavorted in front of them.

Setting down the black bag, Clarence reached in for the first present.

'Jessie McJimpsey,' he shouted in a cheery voice. Little Jessie, attired in party frock, came forward.

'Are you going to be good this Christmas, Jessie?' boomed Santa.

Four-year-old Miss McJimpsey looked Mr Claus in the eye.

'Yes, Mr McGonigall,' she replied.

The room erupted with adult laughter. Santa had been outed.

Jessie was already in Sunday School, and she knew the voice. As soon as she heard Santa speak, she had realised right away that Mr McGonigall was standing in for the real Father Christmas, who was probably preparing for the big day.

After all the presents had been distributed and opened, the children sat around the Christmas tree. As the piano struck up, they joined in the familiar words:

Away in a manger, no crib for a bed,
The little Lord Jesus laid down his sweet head.
The stars in the bright sky looked down where he lay,
The little Lord Jesus asleep on the hay.

During the second verse, Santa Claus looked around the room. He knew almost all of these parents and grandparents. He knew many of their secrets and their fears. He knew how worried they were, like all parents, about the worsening world situation. The glorious new technology, which was supposed to be the liberator of all, had produced in recent years fearsome micro-fusion weapons that even made the old nuclear bombs seem benign by comparison. Who could not be worried for their children and their children's children?

Clarence saw the nostalgia and sadness in their eyes, as they watched the little ones sing with such unaffected trust:

> Be near me, Lord Jesus; I ask thee to stay
> Close by me for ever, and love me, I pray.
> Bless all the dear children in thy tender care,
> And fit us for heaven, to live with thee there.

For all the Christmases he had been a minister, for all the times he had felt he was turning into a mince pie with a dog collar, Clarence never failed to be affected by the singing of children, especially 'Away in a Manger'. Despite its sentimentality—or even because of it—the carol, sung by children, always got to him.

Santa brushed away a tear, and headed back to Scunner manse.

'Aggie, when will Charlie and Beatrice and the kids be arriving?' Clarence asked his wife when he returned.

'They'll be here at tea time,' replied Agnes.

Clarence always enjoyed talking with his elder son, a news reporter with the BBC. They disagreed about lots of things, but they enjoyed these disagreements the way some people enjoy bad health. Neither was short of an opinion or three.

Charlie was different from his younger brother, Angus, a quiet spoken accountant with a droll sense of humour. Angus was spending Christmas at his partner's parents.

'No Christmas card again from Mary,' said Clarence.

'Well, we haven't had one for years,' replied Agnes, 'so it's no great surprise. She wanted to cut herself off, and she's got her wish. We can't force ourselves on her.'

The words cut Clarence to the quick. He had never got used to Mary's chosen absence from their lives.

'I can't help wondering what she's doing, or where she is, Aggie,' said Clarence. 'I wonder if she's still on heroin.'

'I know, Clarence, it's really sad,' said Agnes. 'We don't even know if she's still with that drug-pushing man. I hope not. But I wish she'd get in touch.'

'Hard to believe it's nine years since we saw her,' said Clarence. 'She'll be thirty-nine now. Wonder what she's like.'

He sighed as he put on his coat.

'Where are you going, Clarence?' asked Agnes.

'To Inverness,' he replied. 'I've got two people in hospital. It must be hard to be there at Christmas time. I'll take Squeegee along for the run.'

Squeegee didn't need to be asked twice. She ran, wagging her tail, to the car, and got settled in the passenger seat as usual. She often went with Clarence on pastoral visits, sampling the biscuits at each establishment.

The drive to Inverness took longer than the usual hour and a half because of the snow. Squeegee wagged her tail as her driver sang Christmas carols. She would often howl along when Clarence sang.

'Well, here we are, Squeegee,' said Clarence, as he drove into the hospital car park. 'Thanks for singing the soprano parts. You're better than some of the choir, but don't tell them I said it.'

One of his elders was in a private room in the cancer ward. He was not expected to last long. When Clarence got to the ward, the duty sister told him that Jim was in a coma.

Jim's wife, Jenny, was at the bedside. Clarence sat down beside her, and they remained in silence for some time. Clarence took his elder's hand, and, even though Jim was unconscious, the minister read the familiar words of the 23rd Psalm. Then he laid his hand on Jim's forehead and said a Celtic blessing.

'Jim often disagreed with you, but he was always fond of you, Clarence,' said Jenny, moved. 'Thank you for being such a good friend to him.'

Clarence hugged Jenny, then left the room.

'In the midst of death, we are in life,' muttered Clarence to no one in particular as he moved to the maternity ward.

Santa Claus was in the ward, giving a little gift to each new mother. One of them was Alice McJimpsey, mother of Jessie, the little one who had blown Clarence's cover at the nursery party. Alice's four-hour-old daughter was sleeping at the foot of the bed.

'It's good of you to come all this way to see me on Christmas Eve,' said Alice, shyly.

'Just as well Jessie's not here to see me,' said Clarence. 'Two Santa Clauses in the one room would be a bit confusing.'

Clarence went round the ward, with a word of festive greeting for all of the new mothers. It was when he came to the last bed that he got the shock of his life.

The woman with her baby said to him simply, 'Dad.'

Yes, it was Mary. His Mary. After all these years. He was speechless.

As he bent down to kiss her, his daughter embraced him. 'Dad,' she said, 'I can't believe it's you.'

'And I can't believe it's you, Mary,' said Clarence, choked.

'I'm sorry, dad,' she said. 'It's hard to explain. I've been to places I can't even begin to tell you about.'

'Don't even try,' said Clarence. 'Where's Kenny?'

'He left me when I became pregnant. I came up here from London about two months ago and got a job as a barmaid. I wanted to come and see you and mum, but it was too difficult. I didn't know how to do it. And here you are. My Christmas present.'

'And here's another Christmas present,' said Clarence, pointing to the sleeping bundle. 'Boy or girl?'

'Kenneth,' said Mary. 'But maybe now I'll call him Kenneth James, after you.'

James Clarence McGonigall swelled with pride and affection. This Christmas Eve had taken a miraculous turn.

'Instead of going back to an empty house, why don't you come home with me? You can stay for a day or a week, then never see us again if you don't want to. Charlie and Beatrice and the kids are with us for Christmas.'

'I'm not sure I could handle that,' said Mary. 'I haven't even met the children.'

'It would make Aggie's Christmas,' said Clarence.

'All right,' said Mary, hesitantly. 'I'll come with you.'

'Hail, Mary, full of grace,' said Clarence, softly.

Soon, Mary and the bundled-up Kenneth James were in the back of the car. Squeegee wagged her tail for most of the journey.

At Scunner manse, Clarence bounded out and rang the doorbell. Aggie came to the door.

'Special Christmas delivery,' said Clarence.

Watchnight service. People had crowded into the kirk from pubs and parties, sober, drunk, believing, disbelieving, celebrating, hurting. The air was full of whisky and yearnings. In the back row, near the door, sat a woman with her baby, beside Agnes McGonigall. Nobody knew who the woman was.

Clarence preached like a man inspired. Then the singing of the familiar words:

> Love came down at Christmas,
> Love all lovely, Love Divine;
> Love was born at Christmas,
> Star and angels gave the sign.

During the singing, Clarence heard a familiar howl. Squeegee. She had somehow got herself into the church vestibule. Doing the soprano part again.

At midnight, the lights of the church were dimmed, and Clarence lit a candle. Time seemed to stand still. The corporate yearning was almost tangible as the choir sang,

> Still the night, holy the night!
> Son of God, O how bright
> Love is smiling from thy face!

There were times, if he were honest, when the Reverend J. Clarence McGonigall wasn't sure if he believed in God or not. But not tonight, this special night.

> Strikes for us now the hour of grace,
> Saviour since thou art born!
> Saviour since thou art born!

Despite his frequent, stormy battles with the Church, Clarence knew in his heart what it was that really mattered. The hour of grace, a child of hope.

10. Some Day my Prince Will Come

January. Another year, another compulsory Super-Presbytery training course. The Reverend J. Clarence McGonigall comforted himself with the knowledge that this one would be the last, before he retired in May.

'In the year of Our Lord, 2010,' wrote the Reverend Christopher McFadyen, Convener of the PC Convention, 'We need to be focused on our outcomes. Modern ministers must learn the power of affirmation and visualisation if they are to meet their annual targets. Whatever you visualise will come to be. Visualise yourself with maximum bonus points for baptisms, weddings and funerals at Easter, and that's what you will have. This is the meaning of prayer for our day and age.'

Clarence poured some whisky into his coffee. He knew he needed help to get through this letter.

'This must be Chrimbo's Second Epistle to the Fruitcakes,' he said to Squeegee, his dog, who looked puzzled. She knew the word 'fruitcake', yet none was being offered to her. Sometimes it was hard to be a dog.

'Hey, Aggie, am I the only sane person in this Church?' he shouted to his beloved helpmeet.

'If you are the sanest,' said Agnes as she put her curler-festooned head in the study door, 'then all the others should be in locked wards, and the key thrown away.'

'Aggie, I'm trying to visualise you as Melinda Messenger,' said Clarence, 'but for some reason it isn't working.'

'Clarence, I'm trying to visualise you as a dinosaur, and for some reason it is working,' replied Agnes.

'C'mon, Squeegee,' said Clarence. 'If you can visualise your lead, we'll go somewhere.'

Squeegee trotted off, and came back with the lead in her mouth.

'Well done, Squeegee,' said her master. 'Prepare to meet thy bonus.'

'Before you make a visit in the community, you should visualise the outcome you want,' the Rev Arthur Christopher told the languid, not-so-super presbyters.

'If you're going to visit a young couple, for instance, visualise baptising their child. Your visualisation—along with your repeated affirmation "I am strong, I am in charge"—will bring about the desired outcome.'

Clarence simply had to speak.

'I presume,' said Clarence, 'this means that if you're going to visit an elderly person just when you're near your Easter bonus funeral target, you should visualise smoke coming out of the crematorium chimney.'

The speaker ignored Clarence, but a red flush of anger moved quickly up his neck.

'Modern ministers should practise their visualisations,' Art went on. 'If the Presbyterian Church (Scotland) is to retain market share, and even grow its business, it will need leaders who understand the power of the mind. That is what faith is all about in the twenty-first century.'

'Where there are no visualisations,' muttered Clarence, 'the people perish. May God have mercy on us all.'

Art turned around in a fury, veins sticking out in his temple.

'Mr McGonigall,' he said, 'I am told that you are due to retire in four months. Let me tell you frankly that it can't come soon enough. There will be great rejoicing in Livingston when you finally give up. The progress of the modern church is being held up by rude, reactionary, unreconstructed old pests like you!'

'I am strong, I am in charge,' said Clarence, soothingly. 'Calm down. Breathe slowly and deeply. Visualise a peaceful scene. Now say to yourself, over and over, "I love Clarence McGonigall." You'll be all right soon.'

Despite his rebellion, Clarence, unusually, decided that he would follow the instructions from Livingston. He felt there was nothing to lose.

First stop next day was at the home of old Nancy McCracken. He decided to visualise Nancy offering him a lovely piece of cake. He concentrated very hard on this image.

When Clarence was seated on the couch, Nancy went to put the kettle on. While she was through in the kitchen, Clarence focused his attention on the image of a piece of cherry cake. He imagined it being very succulent. He began to salivate, like one of Pavlov's dogs.

'I am strong, I am in charge,' he intoned.

Nancy came through with the tray.

'Ah ken that ye like ma scones, Mr McGonigall,' she cried.

Scones! This wasn't in the script! The same old scones, like bullets. They always gave Clarence severe indigestion. He did not feel strong and in charge. He felt weak and cheated. He had not visualised scones, but cherry cake. Something had gone wrong! Maybe he hadn't visualised hard enough.

The next visit was to Alex McCrindle, who had resigned from the kirk session after a bitter battle over the decision to move the communion table six inches forward. On his way to the house, Clarence focused on a very peaceful visit. He pictured a serene scene, with goodwill breaking out. This was a real test for Art Christopher's theory.

Clarence knocked at the door, a beatific smile on his face.

'So ye've come at last, have ye?' shouted McCrindle, ushering the minister inside. 'Ah thocht ye were nivver comin'.'

Bad start. Jean McCrindle, who was generally more agreeable than her husband, asked Clarence if he would like a cup of tea. Yes! Maybe this visualisation business was working!

'That communion table will be moved over ma deid body,' said Alex McCrindle.

'I didn't know you wanted to be buried there,' Clarence almost said, but swallowed the words in the interests of peace.

'Our forefaithers spilt their blood tae hiv the communion table exactly whaur it is,' Alex went on.

'Name five people who martyred themselves over the precise siting of the communion table,' Clarence almost said, but didn't.

At this moment, Jean McCrindle came into the living room. Clarence couldn't believe his eyes. He was being offered a piece of cherry cake along with his cup of tea!

Hallelujah! The visualisation had worked—it was simply the timing that was a little out.

'I've just one piece of this nice cake left, and I want you to have it,' said Jean, as her husband scowled.

'I am strong, I am in charge,' Clarence mumbled triumphantly.

Just as he opened his mouth to eat the cake, the living room door burst open. In rushed Prince, the McCrindles' Alsatian, who hurled himself at the minister. As Clarence and his chair flew backwards, the cherry cake soared upwards in an arc. On its descent, it went straight into the open mouth of the grateful dog.

'Call off the hound of hell!' cried Clarence, lying on his back. 'I'll keep the communion table where it is.'

'Ah'm glad ye've changed yer mind,' said McCrindle.

'Only joking,' said Clarence. 'I am strong, I am in charge.'

Still supine, the minister launched into 'All things bright and beautiful', as the hound licked its lips. It had enjoyed the cherry cake.

'Ah think ye're aff yer heid,' said McCrindle.

Visit number three. One last chance. Old Alice Johnston made terrible tea. Clarence visualised a lovely cup of Earl Grey.

When Alice came through from the kitchen, she handed Clarence a beautiful china cup.

'This is a family heirloom,' she told Clarence. 'A special cup for a special minister.'

Clarence beamed, as he lifted the cup to his lips.

The tea was revolting.

'Just a minute,' said Alice, 'I meant to bring you through a scone.'

When Alice disappeared into the kitchen, Clarence looked around desperately. He wondered about pouring the foul liquid into the aspidistra, but decided against it. After all, the poor plant hadn't done anyone any harm. Then he noticed that the window was open.

He rushed over, and threw the tea out of the window. What a relief!

Then, to his horror, he heard a smashing sound below. He looked in disbelief at his hand. Only the handle of the cup was on his finger! The precious family heirloom was in smithereens on the pavement below.

When Alice came in with the scone, the only thing Clarence could say was, 'Do you want your lines now or later?'

'It didn't work,' Clarence told Aggie. By the time he had finished telling his dear wife about his day, tears of laughter streamed down her face.

Five minutes later, she came in—with a cup of Earl Grey tea, and a piece of cherry cake.

'I am strong, I am in charge,' intoned the lady of the manse. 'And don't you forget it.'

11. The McGonigall School of Anger Management

It was the day before the SuperPresbytery's anger management course. In the quiet and peaceable town of Scunner, the only angry person was the Reverend J. Clarence McGonigall, who was furious because he was having to give up three days in order to attend a training event about anger. Nothing put his blood pressure up quite like these compulsory courses full of psychobabble.

So it was not a happy man who got into his car, soon after breakfast. He had to spend so much time in his vehicle that he felt he was a chaplain to a Ford Fiesta. His parish was extensive: and now he had an additional burden in the shape of the interim moderatorship of Snoddy Memorial, linked with Invertottie West, linked with Blethers and Bauchle.

'I'm minister for half of Scotland,' Clarence said to Squeegee, who sat, as usual, on the front passenger seat, 'and they wonder why ministers are angry. And tomorrow I've got to make a round trip of two hundred miles to attend an anger course that'll make us all madder than we were before we started.'

Squeegee wagged her tail. She had heard many rants before, and she was bored by them. She knew, though, that going round the parishes meant scones, so she kept her mind focused on that.

First stop was Inversnecky. Unlike Scunner, the town had a biggish store. Clarence had promised Aggie that he would pick up some food supplies. As he pushed his trolley towards the cheese compartment, he accidentally collided with another shopper.

'Why don't you look where you're going?' she snapped at him. 'You men with trolleys are a complete menace. You should all have to pass a driving test!'

'I'm sorry,' said Clarence.

'So you should be,' the woman, a visitor to Inversnecky, went on. 'You shouldn't be allowed out without a permit. I see that you're a minister, too. You should behave better than this.'

'I'm sorry,' said Clarence, again. 'I didn't mean to bang into you.'

This seemed to make the woman worse. 'Get out of my sight!' she shouted.

'Certainly,' said Clarence.

Next stop, Trachle. Old Ebeneezer McMahon was never the happiest of parishioners. He exemplified P. G. Wodehouse's observation that it was never difficult to distinguish between a Scotsman with a grievance and a ray of sunshine.

'The Kirk isn't what it used to be,' he moaned. 'In my day, people queued for hours just to get into Trachle Kirk for the evening service. Now there is no evening service. In the old days, you saw the minister a lot, but not nowadays. You hardly ever see them. No wonder people don't go to the kirk any more. Mr Thomson, your predecessor, was a fine man. He used to come and see me every two weeks.'

'Ebby, Mr Thomson died of overwork, and he only had Trachle to look after,' said Clarence.

'He was a grand man, just the same,' Stewart droned on, 'not like today's ministers who only work from nine till five. Not only that, in the old days the ministers' wives used to do a lot in the parish, and ran the Guild. They won't do that nowadays.'

Clarence only just managed to keep his temper in check.

More visits, including a dip into Invertottie, produced complaints. Even Squeegee's scone-harvest was poor.

'If I hear the phrase "the good old days" one more time, I think I'll explode,' Clarence told Squeegee on the drive back home. 'Mr Thomson of Trachle certainly must have been a saint—he got through his time without killing Ebeneezer McMahon.'

Squeegee nodded, and concentrated on the prospect of dinner.

Arriving back at Scunner manse, Agnes berated Clarence for being late for tea—again. A man, she said, was waiting for him in the study.

'Mr McGonigall, I've come to tell you that you're not preaching the gospel,' said the stary-eyed stranger. 'The world is coming to an end this year, and you're not preaching about it. The president of China has the mark of the beast upon his head, and there's going to be a big battle between the Chinese and the Americans at Armaggido on the twenty-ninth of November, starting at noon. It's all here in the Book of Revelation, and if you can spare me a few minutes, I'll show you where you're going wrong...'

Clarence bolted down part of his meal, before dashing out to a congregational board meeting in Inversnecky. There was a dispute about whether or not they should replace the worn carpet in the vestry.

'You're supposed to be a neutral chairman,' Angus McPhee, local conspiracy theorist, shouted at Clarence, 'but you're driving this decision.'

Clarence couldn't care less whether the carpet was replaced or not, but he bit his lip. He managed to control himself before bringing the meeting to a close. He needed his bed.

Next morning, before setting off for the Super-Presbytery course, he had to phone about the electricity at the manse. A robotic voice answered: 'You have five choices. If you wish to pay a bill, press one. If you wish to buy one of our products, press two. If you wish to report a fault, press three. If you wish to enrol in our credit club, press four. If you wish to check about an electricity reading, press five.'

'If you wish to have a nervous breakdown, press six,' Clarence shouted, before slamming the phone down, and then jumping into the car.

'Managing your anger is really quite easy,' the Reverend Arthur 'Art' Christopher told the assembled ministers. 'It's all a question of focus. The latest research from America tells us that when you're angry with someone, you should smile. If you smile strongly enough, endorphins will be released in your system, and your feelings will change. You will cease to be angry with them.'

'Did you come all the way from Livingston to tell us this?' asked Clarence McGonigall.

Art smiled at him.

'I suppose that means that you're angry?' said Clarence.

'Yes,' said Art. 'It does. But you can see that I'm managing to keep focus, because I know from past experience that you are a very annoying person, Mr McGonigall. It's all a matter of mind over matter. Anger is very destructive. If you keep smiling, it will go away. Smile with Jesus, in fact, as the motto of our church puts it so well.'

'Doesn't it depend on what you're angry about?' asked Clarence. 'For instance, Isaiah was angry because people turned away from God. Amos was angry because the people of Israel abused the poor and the strangers. Jesus was angry about the money-changers in the temple, and he threw their tables over. He described Herod as a fox, and the Pharisees as hypocrites. No smiling with Jesus there.'

Art's smile was becoming more like a grimace by the minute.

'You know what makes ministers really angry?' Clarence went on. 'It's all the time-wasting stuff we are bombarded with. It's being turned into passive clerks and civil servants. It's being put on short-term contracts and having to meet impossible targets. It's this ridiculous emphasis on marketing and image.

'Want to know how to help ministers to manage their anger? One way would be to get off our backs.'

There was much shuffling of feet, and looking at the ceiling.

'You are one of the great challenges of my life, Mr McGonigall,' said Art Christopher, smiling through gritted teeth.

Driving home from the conference centre, Clarence's mind was racing with all the things he had to do when he got back. As he idled at the traffic lights, he went into a reverie. A loud honking noise broke his thoughts: he had failed to notice that the lights had changed.

The car behind him swerved past, then cut in front of him. As Clarence slammed on his brakes, he noticed that there was a 'Smile with Jesus' sticker on the back of the offending car. The snarling driver was jabbing one finger into the air as he turned round to look at Clarence.

Art Christopher. Clarence beamed at him with a beatific smile, and gave him a wave. Horrified, Art accelerated into the distance.

'Blessed are the meek,' said Clarence. 'It's just as well I've learned how to control my anger.'

Clarence broke into a rendition of 'Yield not to temptation'. Squeegee, as usual, sang the alto part.

12. Terror on the Treadmill with Tanya Hyde

The Reverend J. Clarence McGonigall groaned as he sat at his desk in the study. In fact, that's how he began each day. It was part of a daily liturgy. 'Oh, God,' it always began, followed by what sounded like excerpts from the Book of Lamentations.

The cause of the groaning was the inevitable stack of mail. As always, most of the paperwork was from the headquarters of the Presbyterian Church (Scotland) in Livingston. Clarence complained to God that the community of faith had turned into a law-worshipping civil service which inflicted death by a thousand memos.

'Lord,' he shouted, 'I want to be a minister of the gospel, a preacher, a pastor, not a form-filling, head-counting clerk.' Squeegee wagged her tail. 'Nurses can't get on with nursing because they're deaved to death with paperwork. Doctors can hardly doctor, for filling up endless reports. Teachers can hardly get on with the task of shovelling information into reluctant bairns. Farmers spend more time shuffling documents than shovelling dung. The lunatics have taken over the asylum.'

Squeegee nodded her head. She was used to these morning expositions. She often howled as her master exhorted the Lord to spare him any more nonsense. It was Presbyterian choral morningsong.

Clarence had once sent a letter to Livingston, complaining about the volume of mail. In it, he had quoted a missive from the Duke of Wellington to the Secretary of State for War in 1810: 'My Lords, if I attempted to answer the mass of futile correspondence that surrounds me, I should be debarred from all serious business of campaigning. I must remind your Lordships, for the last time, that so long as I hold an independent position, I shall see to it that no officer under my command is debarred, by attending to this futile drivelling of mere quill driving in your Lordships' office, from attending to his first duty, which is always to train the private soldiers under his command. Your obedient servant, Wellington.'

In their reply, the Livingston mullahs had threatened to reduce Clarence's bonuses. He cast his eye again over the pile of envelopes.

'How long, O Lord, how long?' cried Clarence.

'Till May, you auld grump,' cackled his wife Agnes, as she stuck her head—adorned with curlers—in the study doorway. 'That's when you retire. Have you forgotten already? It's time you were taken into care. I think I'll phone Livingston and tell them their favourite minister has finally lost the plot.'

'I knew I should have married Brigitte Bardot when I had the chance,' responded Clarence.

'I presume it was the prospect of Scunner manse that put her off,' replied Aggie. 'If it hadn't been for that, she would have leapt into the arms of the Don Juan of Inversnecky.

'Anyway, isn't it time you stopped moaning about these nice people in Livingston, Clarence? You blame them for everything, from the spread of mad cow disease among ministers to the collapse of western Christendom. And why are you complaining about all this to God? He must go straight into a coma every time you start.'

Worsted yet again, Clarence opened the first letter. It had the familiar yellow Mr Happy and the 'Smile with Jesus!' slogan along the top. How Clarence hated that image! All clergy had been given free Mr Happy stickers to put on their cars, but he had resolutely refused. Instead, he put a hand-done message on the rear of his old, stuttering, banger which read, 'This car is God's way of telling you to slow down'. Irate motorists would honk at him—even in Inversnecky—but he would simply wave cheerfully in response.

'Missive number three million, three thousand, three hundred and three from the palace of laughter in Livingston,' muttered Clarence, as he started to read the letter. 'This is what they do to while away the weary hours till the Second Coming.'

The letter said he and Aggie had to attend a compulsory residential retirement course.

It was held at Crieff Hydro. Clarence, who had enjoyed many holidays there with Aggie, was old enough to remember the days when there was no licence at the Hydro. Ministers—who got cheap rates out of season—used to drink sherry in wardrobes. It lent a cloak-and-dagger air to the holiday. There was an unmistakable sense of daring in the air.

It was announced that each minister had to have an individual physical training session in the gym. The Reverend Tanya Hyde, whose job at the Livingston HQ was that of whipping ministers into line and administering the ministers' performance-related pay scheme, was in charge.

'We must make sure you're fit for your retirement, Mr McGonigall,' said Tanya, with a smile.

At long last, she had this nuisance, this thorn in the flesh, this complete pain, exactly where she wanted him. She had been looking forward to this for months.

Clarence protested that he didn't have a tracksuit.

'No problem,' said Tanya, cheerfully. 'I've got one for you.'

She certainly did. It was just like hers—dark blue trousers and top, with a big, yellow, Mr Happy figure above the big slogan, 'Smile with Jesus!'

Gotcha!

'I think we'll start on the treadmill,' said Tanya. 'This will hurt you more than it hurts me.'

'What if I refuse to run on this thing?' said Clarence.

'It's Easter next month. Bonuses.'

Knowing what Aggie would have said about that, Clarence got on to the machine. Tanya pressed the button, and the treadmill began to roll, slowly. Clarence started walking, then running as it speeded up. He had to; the only other option was to fall off. He tried to look defiant, but only succeeded in looking ridiculous.

'You're doing well, Mr McGonigall,' said Tanya. 'Do you run for the Inversnecky Harriers?'

She was enjoying this. She would also enjoy telling her colleagues at the Livingston headquarters. She turned the treadmill up a notch or two.

'Are you trying to kill me?' asked Clarence, plaintively.

'Now, why would I want to do a thing like that?' replied Tanya, sweetly. 'You're doing so well, I think I'll speed it up a bit.'

'Were you once married to the Marquis de Sade?' gasped Clarence, running faster.

'Smile with Jesus!' replied Tanya.

Suddenly, there were great screams of laughter. Clarence didn't even need to look. Aggie had sneaked into the gym to see what was going on. The sight of her red-faced, puffing husband, running on a treadmill, dressed in a tracksuit with 'Smile with Jesus!' emblazoned on it, was all too much. She rolled on the floor, kicking her legs in the air, hooting with laughter.

'I can't believe this sight!' she screeched. 'Clarence doing what someone from Livingston tells him, running on a treadmill, wearing a "Smile with Jesus" top—this must be mentioned in the book of Revelation!'

Tanya Hyde looked in amazement. Clarence kept running, running. Aggie fled the gym, helpless with mirth.

'It looks like Livingston has tamed you at long last, Mr McGonigall,' Tanya said triumphantly.

'Over my dead body,' gasped Clarence.

'If you prefer it that way,' said Tanya.

Suddenly, Clarence bounced off the treadmill, and crumpled in a heap, motionless.

'Oh, no!' shouted Tanya, rushing over to him. Getting no response, she began to give him the kiss of life. 'Don't die on me!' she gasped.

Clarence cocked an eyebrow. 'No, you wouldn't want to lose your number one minister, would you? Tanya, we must stop meeting like this.'

'You swine!' screamed Tanya.

'The trouble with the new puritan army is that it has no sense of humour,' replied Clarence.

'You're incorrigible!' shouted Tanya, veins sticking out in her temple. 'Thank goodness you're retiring in May. People like you are obstructing the recovery of the Church after the modern surgery it needed.'

'The operation was successful, but the patient is dying,' said Clarence, quietly. 'It's the Church which needs the kiss of life.'

Back at Scunner, people had to get used to an unusual sight. Their parish minister, a very late convert to exercise, was running through the streets, with his dog, Squeegee, at his heels. Clarence wore his tracksuit, with 'Smile with Jesus!' on it.

'What a wonderful slogan!' one man shouted from a crowd of admirers. 'It's a great witness!'

'Post-modern irony,' responded Clarence.

But, as usual, nobody had a clue what this mad old character was on about.

13. Stranger on the Shore

Holy Week, 2010. The Reverend J. Clarence McGonigall felt a little sad, knowing that this would be his last Easter as minister of Inversnecky North, linked with Scunner South, linked with Trachle (Continuing), linked with Havers Memorial.

'I'm not looking forward to this, Aggie,' he told his wife, who had commented on his sombre demeanour. 'The people here have been good to me. I've been through a lot with them. It's hard to believe that this will be the last Holy Week and Easter here. I'll miss the people.'

'The people at the church headquarters will miss you as well,' said Agnes. 'They'll miss your charm, and your diplomacy, and your humble obedience. They'll have a service to mark your retirement next month.'

Clarence ignored his wife's tongue-in-cheek comments. He knew as well as Agnes did that any service in Livingston would be one of thanksgiving for the unblessed departed.

'I'd like this Holy Week to be special,' said Clarence. 'I want it to be memorable.'

Clarence always found Holy Week both chastening and exhilarating. Chastening because, as he moved meditatively each year through the events of Christ's last week, he was brought face to face with his own lack of commitment, his betrayals, his despair, his faithlessness, his personal inadequacies. Exhilarating, because beyond his own frailties lay a transforming power which was not of this world.

Clarence had been sent worship material from the Marketing Department—which had replaced the old Department of National Mission—of the Presbyterian Church (Scotland). With a picture of a dancing Mr Happy on the front cover, the glossy booklet was titled *Positive Thinking for Holy Week*.

Inside were 'Seven Habits of Positive Presbyterians'. Each Top Tip For Happiness—such as 'Start each day with fruit juice and a prayer!'—was accompanied by a picture of a smiling Presbyterian. The five from North America had gleaming, white teeth. The two Scots had slightly discoloured dentures.

Under the headline 'Positive Thinking about the Crucifixion', one testimony by a Christian entrepreneur said that while hearing a Good Friday reading in church, he had conceived the idea of manufacturing large plastic figures of Jesus on a plastic cross, illumined by a flashing neon light. Millions had been sold. Even President Jeb Bush had endorsed the product, going on national television to encourage Christians to put them in their windows as the country waged war against Pakistan.

'Oh, God, save us,' said Clarence.

Palm Sunday. How Clarence loved Palm Sunday! As usual, Jock Fletcher, a local farmer, provided the minister with a donkey. The procession of children, followed by adults, began in Inversnecky town centre.

> Hosannah, loud hosannah,
> The little children sang;
> Through pillared court and temple
> The joyful anthem rang.

The Inversnecky Town Band led the praise, not always hitting the right notes but giving the singers courage. Clarence never failed to be affected by the Palm Sunday songs, with their mixture of jubilation, foreboding and yearning. The knowledge that the shouts of gospel praise would turn to cries for blood before the week was out pierced Clarence McGonigall's heart.

> Ride on, ride on in majesty!
> The winged squadrons of the sky
> Look down with sad and wondering eyes
> To see the approaching sacrifice.

The fickleness of the crowd! The hairs stood out on the back of the minister's neck as the congregation sang:

> Sometimes they strew his way,
> And his sweet praises sing
> Resounding all the day hosannas to their king.
> Then 'Crucify!' is all their breath
> And for his death they thirst and cry.

The drumbeat of Holy Week had begun.

Maundy Thursday. The Son of Man goeth as it is written of him: but woe unto that man by whom the Son of Man is betrayed! It had been good for that man if he had not been born. Then Judas, which betrayed him, answered and said, Master, is it I? He said unto him, Thou hast said. And as they were eating, Jesus took bread, and blessed it, and brake it, and gave it to the disciples, and said, Take, eat, this is my body. And he took the cup, and gave thanks, and gave it to them, saying, Drink ye all of it.

In Trachle, Clarence shared a footwashing service with the local Episcopal rector, Ben Carruthers. They both washed the feet of the twenty or so members of the congregation, then celebrated Holy Communion.

> 'Twas on that night when doomed to know
> The eager rage of every foe,
> That night in which he was betrayed,
> The Saviour of the world took bread.

There was something about the simplicity of the service which moved Clarence. He was feeling emotional about leaving his congregation, and the words of the Gospel story, moving inexorably to their climax, touched him deeply. But there was another sadness within him, one which he could not identify.

Then cometh Jesus with them unto a place called Gethsemane, and saith unto the disciples, Sit ye here, while I go and pray yonder. And he took with him Peter and the two sons of Zebedee, and began to be sorrowful and very heavy. Then saith he unto them, My soul is exceeding sorrowful, even unto death: tarry ye here, and watch with me. And he went a little farther, and fell on his face, and prayed, saying, O my Father, if it be possible, let this cup pass from me: nevertheless not as I will, but as thou wilt.

The die is cast.

Good Friday. When he saw the two policemen at the door of Scunner Manse, the Reverend J. Clarence McGonigall said simply, 'If it be possible, let this cup pass from me.'

'Can we come in, Clarence?' said Sergeant Angus Crichton. He was an elder at Havers. The minister led them into the study.

'Angus,' he said, 'Is it about Mary?'

'I'm afraid it is,' said the sergeant. 'There's no nice way of saying this, Clarence. She was found dead this morning.'

Dead. His daughter. Mary. Yet somehow he knew.

'What happened?' asked Clarence, though there would be no surprises.

'Heroin overdose,' replied Crichton.

'What about the child?' asked Clarence.

'A neighbour has him. He's safe and well.'

'I wish we could have done more for Mary...' said the minister.

'You couldn't have, Clarence,' replied the policeman. 'Don't torture yourself. You've helped so many people find forgiveness and peace, now it's your turn.'

Angus Crichton pulled a black book from his pocket. It was not his police notebook, but a small Bible. He opened it at Psalm 55, and read the words: 'Cast thy burden upon the Lord, and he shall sustain thee.'

Clarence wept.

'Angus,' Clarence said to the sergeant, 'you are a minister to me in my need. You are the healer now. My time here has not been in vain.'

As the two policemen left, Agnes McGonigall came back from the shops. She looked at the officers, a question forming on her lips.

'Come in, Aggie,' said Clarence. 'I think you'd better sit down.'

When she saw the tears in his eyes, she knew immediately what had happened.

'Well,' said Agnes, 'you said that you wanted this Holy Week to be special, one to remember.'

Now from the sixth hour there was darkness over all the land unto the ninth hour. And about the ninth hour, Jesus cried with a loud voice, saying, Eli, Eli, lama sabachthani? That is to say, My God, my God, why hast thou forsaken me?

There had been a reconciliation with Mary at Christmas time, when her son was born. But gripped by addiction and deserted by her drug-dealing partner when she became pregnant, Mary had retreated to inward places that Clarence and Agnes simply could not reach. Their daughter's despair was compounded by feelings of shame and unworthiness, culminating in this terrible, terminal Black Friday.

Clarence would have exchanged his life for Mary's if he could. He had had his time, but his daughter's life had been too short, even though she looked older than her years. He understood for the first time that the growing sense of foreboding he had experienced this Holy Week had not just been related to the closing sequence of the life of Jesus, but to another drumbeat of impending death, far outside his consciousness.

His eye fell upon the dancing Mr Happy. Would the Seven Habits of Positive Presbyterians save him? Would the Top Tips For Happiness ease his despair? Or might Positive Thinking about the Crucifixion be just the thing for this Good/Bad Friday?

He caught sight again of the plastic, neon-lit Jesus, on his cross. 'My God, my God, why hast thou forsaken me?' sighed Clarence, as he threw the booklet on to his overflowing bin.

Holy Saturday. The day of waiting, the day of making a grave with the wicked. Clarence took from the shelves one of his favourite theological books, *Between Cross and Resurrection: a Theology of Holy Saturday*, by Alan Lewis, a man he had known and admired. He read again the words he had underlined: 'We have not really listened to the gospel story of the cross and grave until we have construed this cold, dark sabbath as the day of atheism. For now, the solitary sounds to be heard are throaty cries of triumph from the world's satanic despots, and strangulated wails of disbelief from their indignant, disillusioned victims.'

For Clarence McGonigall, this last Holy Saturday in his parish was a day of desolation and yearning. Lord, I believe. Help thou mine unbelief.

Easter Sunday. Clarence had insisted on taking the Easter communion service. Grieving or not, he simply had to preach his last Easter sermon at Scunner. Not only that, he knew within himself that if his sometimes faltering Easter faith had to mean anything, the time was now.

Neither he nor Agnes slept that night. Abandoning the hope of slumber, they got up and had a cup of tea. Having learned that Kenny, Mary's partner, had declared that he wanted nothing to do with the upbringing of his son—indeed was in no fit state to be involved—Clarence and Agnes talked the matter through. They determined that they would bring up Kenneth James.

'Just as well I'm retiring next month,' said James Clarence McGonigall. 'I'll need to remember how to change nappies.'

'Remember!' exclaimed Aggie. 'How can you remember how to do something you've never done in your life!'

Clarence had no sermon prepared. At 6am, he decided to go out for a walk along the seashore in order to get his fragile head together. So many things were buzzing in his brain that he felt light-headed. He hoped he would be able to cope in the pulpit in a few hours time.

Light was starting to filter through the shadowy darkness. In his disorientated state, he almost collided with a figure emerging from the shadows.

'Sorry,' said Clarence.

'Death is not the last word,' said the stranger, quietly. 'Love has no ending.'

Clarence turned around, but the stranger was no longer visible. The minister went after him, but the man was running in the shadows. No, he seemed to be dancing on the shore.

Clarence wondered if he was hallucinating. Or was he just exhausted?

Jesus saith unto her, Woman, why weepest thou? Whom seekest thou? She, supposing him to be the gardener, saith unto him, Sir, if thou hast borne him hence, tell me where thou has laid him, and I will take him away. Jesus saith unto her, Mary. She turned herself, and saith unto him, Rabboni; which is to say, Master.

Death is not the last word. Love has no ending.

Yes, affirmed Clarence McGonigall, unbelieving believer, wounded healer. Yes.

14. Kentucky Fried Religion: for the Sake of Auld Lang Syne

This is it. Today, at the convention of the Presbyterian Church (Scotland) in Livingston, the Reverend J. Clarence McGonigall will formally retire as minister of Inversnecky North, linked with Scunner South, linked with Trachle (Continuing), linked with Havers Memorial.

Before heading for the Livingston bus, Clarence walks around central Edinburgh on a nostalgic journey. He wanders down to Holyrood, where, as a minister of the old Church of Scotland, he had attended many garden parties. Then he takes a tour of the Scottish parliament building, which had opened in 2004 at a cost of £500 million.

'Nice building, pity about the inhabitants,' Clarence jokes to the guide, who stares back at him without smiling. Clarence isn't overimpressed by the coalition government of Scottish Nationalists and Liberal Democrats, led by First Minister Nicola Sturgeon.

He walks up the Royal Mile to the old Assembly Hall. He stands in the quadrangle, looking up at the statue of the stern-faced John Knox. As a radical young student

he was a critic of Knox; now he is a defender of the Scottish Reformer against the monstrous regiment of marketing modernisers.

Clarence walks up the stairs and into what was the old General Assembly hall. It is now a lapdancing club. Tables are arranged around the sides, and in the centre is a stage, with a pole reaching up to the roof.

As the minister stands there, he hears echoes of past tempestuous debates, from times when the old Church of Scotland addressed national and international concerns. He pictures in his mind's eye the packed galleries, as the Kirk discussed the state of Africa, and as George MacLeod and James Pitt-Watson argued passionately and eloquently about nuclear weapons.

Clarence's reverie is disturbed by the presence of a scantily-clad young woman. She is auditioning for a role in the nightly dramas which are enacted before the lascivious patrons.

'Are you part of the cabaret?' she asks the dog-collared man, with endearing innocence.

'Life is a cabaret,' replies Clarence.

'Oh,' says the girl.

'Is your show called "Opportunity Knox"?' asks Clarence.

The girl stares at the minister, mystified. She has not the slightest idea what this crazy old man is talking about.

Down the Mound, along Princes Street. The shops are almost all American chain stores. Clarence hurries into George Street and stands outside Number 121, the old Kirk's offices, now the Scottish headquarters of Kentucky Fried Chicken.

'Pax Americana,' he says, loudly. 'They call it peace, but they have created a dessert—a Texas doughnut with cream. Thus are we unmanned by Empire.'

An Edinburgh matron looks worriedly at the strange, mumbling figure, then hurries on past.

Next door is a religious book store, the only link with Presbyterian days. Clarence goes in.

He looks at the books. There are titles like *My Dog Came Home Speaking in Tongues—Did Yours?* and

Making Profits with Jesus. He picks up a paperback called *The Submissive Christian Wife*.

'I think I'll get this one for Aggie,' mutters Clarence, 'though I've a feeling it's too late.'

Music pours forth from the speakers. It is the chart-topping revival of the Lord's Prayer, to the tune of 'Auld Lang Syne', by Sir Cliff Richard.

'If you don't turn that off, I'll top myself,' Clarence says to one of the assistants. The young woman looks alarmed. Her training has not prepared her for a threatened suicide. She decides to play safe and smile sweetly.

'Can I help you with anything?' she inquires.

'Do you have the biography of Archie Craig?' asks Clarence.

'Who?' replies the woman.

'Do you have *The Epistle to the Romans*, by Karl Barth?' asks Clarence.

'Who?' replies the woman.

'Aaaaargh!' says the Reverend Clarence McGonigall, 'It is finished.'

The Reverend Christopher 'Chrimbo' McFadyen announces the opening praise at the start of the Convention of the Presbyterian Church (Scotland). It is 'If you love Jesus, stamp your feet'. The delegates dutifully stamp their feet at the appropriate points.

The singing of the metrical psalms had ended when the old Church of Scotland was privatised. They were deemed to be 'lacking relevancy' by the Committee Anent the Modernising of the Church.

'Give me a break,' mutters Clarence, who finds the invitation to stamp his feet if he loves Jesus to be perfectly resistible.

Chrimbo, wearing designer jeans, open-necked silk shirt, and religious designer-jewellery, calls the Convention to prayer.

'Lord, we just want to thank you that you have called us here to Livingston,' he begins. 'We just want to say how happy we are. We just want to say that we are just Smiling with Jesus! In fact we just want to tell you that we are just so pleased. It just feels good.'

'And the Lord just wants to puke,' declares a loud voice. Delegates turn and stare at the aged troubler of the ecclesiastical waters. Clarence is undeterred.

'The liturgical barbarians are not just at the gates, they have taken over the citadel,' he goes on. 'This is Opportunity Knox for five-year-olds. If this is progress, God help us all.'

The Rev Tanya Hyde comes to the microphone, to give a report on the ministers' bonus scheme.

'I am pleased to say that the strategy of putting ministers on short-term contracts, reducing the basic wage, and paying annual performance-related bonuses has proved an outstanding success,' she says. 'We have been successful in creating a ministry of high achievers.

There are one or two exceptions, of course, and we will name and shame them, but the vast majority have increased the number of baptisms, weddings and funerals year on year.'

The Convention then breaks into the song, 'If you're happy and you know it', with the words displayed on huge screens.

'Doesn't it make you feel good?' shouts Chrimbo. 'Hug people round about you! We're a church that is going places!'

'I know where I'm going,' says Clarence, heading for the exit. He is held back by his friend, Gavin McAllister.

Next, Clarence is called to the microphone by Chrimbo.

'One of our beloved brethren leaves us today,' says Chrimbo. 'As is our custom, we will ask our retiring friend, Clarence McGonigall, to make a very short speech. At church headquarters, we are so sorry to see Mr McGonigall go.'

There is an uneasy silence as the minister stands on the rostrum.

'Moderator,' he begins, 'I mean, Convener. The headquarters of the Church are not in Livingston. They are in every parish in our land, and in this Assembly— even though it has been turned into a sales rally.

'It has been my privilege to be a minister of the gospel. The purpose of the Church is to be faithful to that gospel. Its task is not to produce sales figures and marketing gimmicks, but to cultivate holiness.'

'You have one minute left,' interjects Chrimbo.

'Some people think I'm against change,' Clarence continues. 'I'm not. Of course the Church has to reform itself, but mimicking the worst lunacies of the finance-driven world around us is not reform. It is surrender to false gods.'

A bell goes. Chrimbo tells Clarence his time is up.

'In the Church, we have been mesmerised by management-speak,' Clarence continues. 'Despite the "Church Without Walls" report nine years ago, power has been gathered to the administrative centre. The ministry of word and sacrament has been reduced to a religious civil service. This is the Babylonian captivity of our day...'

Clarence's voice trails away. Chrimbo has cut off his microphone.

The Reverend J. Clarence McGonigall sits on the bus heading out of Livingston. In a matter of hours, he will be back with Aggie, and Squeegee. He will be amongst his congregation, who have been repeatedly maddened and inspired by the minister they love. They will say their farewells. There will be tears.

As he munches one of Aggie's sandwiches, Clarence is at peace with himself, despite his frustrations. God has been good to him. He is happy and he knows it: and he does not need to stamp his feet.

15. Farewell to a Retiring Friend

Ron Ferguson's year-long series of tales in *Life & Work* about the Reverend J. Clarence McGonigall, legendary minister of Inversnecky North, linked with Scunner South, linked with Trachle (Continuing), linked with Havers Memorial, has come to an end. To satisfy insatiable worldwide curiosity, *Life & Work* outbid *Hello* magazine to publish an exclusive conversation between Mr McGonigall and Mr Ferguson.

JC McG: Tell me, Ron, why did you create me?

RF: For money, really.

JC McG: Money! Surely there was something more honourable than that at stake? Surely you wanted to show a great Reformer at work?

RF: Nope.

JC McG: C'mon, Ron...

RF: If you want to know how it all began, I'll tell you. I dreamed you up, as a one-off. You were so popular

that it was decided to keep you alive. The rest, as they say, is hysteria.

JC McG: Why just a year, though? Surely I could run forever?

RF: Maybe you could, but I couldn't. The trick, Clarence, is to stop when you're on top. It seems that people are still enjoying your adventures, but you could become a bit of a bore, you know.

JC McG: There were rumours which reached as far as Scunner that one or two people wanted to kill me off, early on.

RF: My lips are sealed.

JC McG: What would prise them open?

RF: Money.

JC McG: I see, you're just a mercenary, then.

RF: No more than you are, Clarence. You sold your principles for a mess of Easter bonuses.

JC McG: That's not fair. The people at Livingston made us all sign contracts that gave us a very low basic wage, supplemented by bonuses for baptisms, marriages and funerals. I owed it to Aggie to bring home a reasonable wage. Whenever I rebelled too much, church headquarters put the squeeze on my small but perfectly formed bonuses. Aggie would have killed me if I had come home with less money. I pulled my horns in for the love of a good woman.

RF: Ah, cherchez la femme. It's always the woman's fault, isn't it? On another matter, Clarence, lots of readers have asked me why you named your dog Squeegee.

JC McG: But it was you who called her Squeegee.

RF: Oh yes, I forgot.

JC McG: So why did you call her Squeegee?

RF: Because I once had a dog called Squeegee. She was a lovely mongrel who walked sideways and looked like a mop. I wanted to give her a new life. Are you happy with her?

JC McG: Yes. Everybody in the parish loves her. They feed her with scones and biscuits. Now that I've retired, the congregation will miss her. Now here's a question for you. I've had letters from readers, too, and they ask me whether you and I are exactly the same.

RF: Heaven forbid!

JC McG: What are the differences?

RF: Where do I begin? For a start, you are absolutely useless with technology. You still haven't mastered the computer, and you threw your mobile phone into a grave, remember? I really enjoy my computer, and I find my mobile to be very handy.

JC McG: I think you're underestimating the negative power of technology. Everybody seems to be in thrall to it. If the devil had wanted to ensnare ministers, he couldn't have planned it better—locked up in their studies, glued to a flickering screen, filling up endless forms for church headquarters. And mobile phones are a complete menace. You can't go anywhere without these intrusive pests. Train journeys, which used to be such a pleasure, are a nightmare nowadays. I think you've been seduced by new technologies. It's time you read Jacques Ellul.

RF: He was a bit of a pessimist, wasn't he?

JC McG: A realist, Ronboy, a realist. And a prophet for our time. Read him if you can tear yourself away from your beloved computer. So what are the other differences between us?

RF: I think you're too resistant to change. The Church always needs to change and adapt to meet new situations. You're a bit of an old reactionary. You were reluctant to be reformed.

JC McG: Whoah! I did the visualisations, didn't I? And the anger management course? And I went for a makeover. I'm not against change as such. Of course the Church needs a new reformation. The trouble is that this is being confused with committee reorganisation and management-speak. With our bonuses, and marketing talk and positive thinking and obsession with gadgets and fixation on success, we've created a false gospel. That's why I oppose all this junk!

RF: But aren't you being unreasonable, Clarence? You blame everything on the church headquarters in Livingston. Isn't this just pathetic? Even Aggie agrees with me. These good people are only doing their job. Isn't it time you grew up and realised that nothing is black and white?

JC McG: You're talking rubbish. Of course there are a lot of decent people in Livingston, but what we're seeing is too much centralised power being exercised by officials and department leaders. We've watched while ministers of word and sacrament have been transformed into civil servants and apparatchiks on short-term contracts and payment-by-results. We've stood by while the old General Assembly was turned into a stage-managed sales convention. We've said nothing when dissent was dismissed as disloyalty. We've elevated being 'nice' into the prime Christian virtue, at the expense of truthfulness. We kow-tow to royalty. We're a disgrace to John Knox.

RF: But do you have to be such a crabbit old grumbler?

JC McG: Yes.

RF: Oh, well, as long as Squeegee loves you.

JC McG: Now let me ask you something, Ron. Some of my fan club...

RF: You mean the Reverend J. Clarence McGonigall has groupies?

JC McG: Yes. Are you jealous? Some of my fan club have asked me whether you were trying to prophesy with these stories.

RF: The answer is no. I wasn't trying to predict that Ann Widdecombe would become prime minister or even that the Church would turn out the way I described it. I was warning about temptations when the Church is up against it. But you did stick a pie in Ann Widdecombe's face, didn't you?

JC McG: If you say so.

RF: Take responsibility for your actions!

JC McG: Another question from my loyal readers: are people like Art Christopher, Chrimbo McFadyen, Nancy Kirk and Tanya Hyde based on real people?

RF: No. I know a lot of readers have had fun trying to match these characters up, but any resemblance to other persons, living, dead or half dead is in the eye of the beholder.

JC McG: Talking about the eye of the beholder, I think I'm better looking than your artist made me. Who is he anyway?

RF: Bill McArthur from the island of Sanday in Orkney, and I think he got you just right. He's the best in the business.

JC McG: Do you think you'll write about me again?

RF: Unlikely. Sane readers can only take so much.

JC McG: Must go now to meet Aggie. Last question: I know you believe I'm a batty old grump, but do you think I've any redeeming features?

RF: Lots. You know what I like about you, Clarence? Underneath all your crazed absurdities, you're a good man. You've stood up for the ministry of word and sacrament as an independent vocation, with the pastoral and the prophetic at its core. You've confronted the powers that want to turn the ministry into a great bureaucracy of clerks...

JC McG: You know, Ronboy, you do sound a bit pompous sometimes.

RF: So be it. Anyway, Clarence, it's been nice knowing you. Give a big hug to Aggie, and a pat on the heid to Squeegee. You know, I've grown to love you all. Maybe now you've retired, you'll be less of a crusty old curmudgeon!

JC McG: In your dreams.

RF: That's where you began, Clarence.

Afterword

A cynical definition of an editor is someone who is paid to separate the wheat from the chaff, and then print the chaff. Like most former editors, if I am honest I can look back with regret at some of the chaff I published. But I can also look back with pleasure and pride at some good things that I managed to do. To the fore among these good things was launching Ron Ferguson's career as a columnist on *The Herald* in 1997.

It was thus a special bonus for me, a few years later, during my brief stint as interim editor of *Life & Work*, to be able to cajole Ron into embarking on a series of short stories for the magazine. I had little idea that I was helping to unleash J. Clarence McGonigall on an unsuspecting world. Yet Clarence—crabbit, cussed but ultimately compassionate and on the side of the angels—rapidly built up his adoring army of fans.

Clarence is a consummate creation. I suspect that the trick lies in Ron's treatment of him, which verges on sentimentality without quite falling into sheer mawkishness. What gives the stories their zest and their edge is the satire: Ron uses Clarence to tilt, with devastating effect, at a church which is being hijacked by pseudo-modernisers, power-crazed bureaucrats and trendy evangelists. Couldn't happen to our beloved Kirk? Well, I sincerely hope not, and so does Ron. But the danger signals are there for all to see.

Alas, Clarence is to be with us no more. But this excellent collection ensures that he will live on for many years yet, and his many admirers will be able to relive his adventures whenever the mood takes them. And the good news is that Ron—no mean minister himself, and also biographer, community leader, columnist and of course short story writer—is to venture into exciting new creative pastures. I understand that, among other things, he is writing both a play and a historical novel. And I am delighted that Lynne Robertson has persuaded him to keep writing for *Life & Work*, albeit in another format. There seems no end to the maestro's fecundity; long may his pen flourish.

Harry Reid
Edinburgh
February 2003